Hell Fire in Paradise

Laurel Baker lost her husband and her two boys on the same day. Then, as if that wasn't enough, logging magnate Robert Dunn came riding to her ranch on Paradise Creek with gunmen at his side and a cold sneer on his face, offering to buy her out.

Naturally, Laurel refuses to sell the place where her loved ones lay buried, but Dunn won't take no for an answer and he soon turns to shooting to get his way. Laurel has the help of her loyal friends but will that be enough when Dunn brings ten deadly gunmen along for the final battle for her land? Can she live through hell-fire in Paradise?

Hell Fire in Paradise

Chuck Tyrell

A Black Horse Western

ROBERT HALE · LONDON

© Chuck Tyrell 2010
First published in Great Britain 2010

ISBN 978-0-7090-9012-0

Robert Hale Limited
Clerkenwell House
Clerkenwell Green
London EC1R 0HT

www.halebooks.com

For Janice, who dreamed the dream

Typeset by
Derek Doyle & Associates, Shaw Heath
Printed and bound in Great Britain by
CPI Antony Rowe, Chippenham and Eastbourne

CHAPTER ONE

Jimmy Baker complained. 'But Ma, it's hardly dark. I'm five now. I don't need to go to bed so early.'

'I know, son. But tomorrow will come before you know it, and I want you in bed right now. Jason's in the loft and asleep already, and you should be, too.'

'Ah, Ma. How come I have to go to bed so early all the time?'

Laurel Baker chuckled at her sturdy son's resistance. 'Unless you get enough sleep, you won't grow big and strong like Pa. And if you don't grow big and strong, how are you going to help on the ranch?'

'OK. I'm going. But I'll stay up when I get bigger, I surely will.' Grumbling, the youngster climbed the ladder into the boys' private bedroom in the loft under the eaves.

Laurel put the youngsters to bed right after supper for good reason. Jack Baker took the wagon into Ponderosa for supplies that morning, and he'd not returned. A knot settled into the pit of Laurel's stomach. Jack didn't run late. He didn't go to Bogtown to drink and he wasn't one to waste time jawing. He might need assistance, but the road from Ponderosa to Paradise was little travelled. If Jack needed help, Laurel had to provide it. She waited until the boys were asleep, changed into a cutdown pair of Jack's old jeans, and stomped her feet into her riding boots. Laurel saddled her steeldust gelding, Angel, and rode toward Ponderosa with a Yellow Boy Winchester in her hands.

Paradise Creek tumbled through a malpais gorge at least a hundred feet deep and the mail road to Alpine travelled the gorge's edge for a good five miles after crossing the plateau from Ponderosa. The wagon track to Paradise branched off the mail road just beyond Sheepshead promontory. Laurel cantered Angel up the wagon track and onto the mail road. She guided the gelding along the road at a trot as deep wagon-wheel ruts made the footing precarious for a running horse. Clouds backed up against Mt Baldy and Mt Ord, covering the sky for miles north of Paradise. The dark night made tracking impossible so Laurel could only hope that if Jack needed help, he was out in the open where she could find him. In the dark night, she felt uneasy, and jacked a shell into the chamber of the Yellow Boy.

Laurel rode more than halfway to Ponderosa but found no trace of Jack. Despondent, she turned Angel around and trotted him back along the mail road toward the Rafter P ranch in Paradise. Jack could take care of himself. He never wore a gun in Ponderosa and didn't drink, so the chance of a random gunfight was next to none. Yet she worried. Jack wouldn't stay away from the ranch all night without good reason. A crippled horse. A broken wagon tongue. A rim separated from a wheel. Something. She turned off to follow the wagon track back to the ranch. Tears burned at the corners of her eyes. No. She could depend on Jack. In their six years together, he'd never let her down. Jack would be home. Laurel raised her head and took a deep breath. He would be home. He would.

Jack and Laurel built their house above Paradise Creek on a small rise that looked out across the valley, which also bore the name of Paradise. From their knoll, the Bakers could see three miles or more downstream when the weather was clear. Laurel peered toward the house, not that she could see it on such a dark night. An orange-red flicker caught her attention. Had she left a lamp on? Fire? A new fear blossomed in her heart. Fire! Jimmy and Jason were in the loft. No one to wake them. No one to carry them from danger. Laurel shoved the Winchester into its scabbard and raked her spurs across Angel's ribs. The startled horse hit a dead run in three strides. Laurel leaned over his neck, urging him on, her eyes on the orange-red glare that gradually got brighter as the gelding plunged on.

By the time they reached the burning house, Angel was streaked with lather and Laurel's cheeks were streaked with tears.

'Jimmy! Jason!' She screamed her children's names, but only the roar of the fire replied. Smoke poured from the chimney and seeped out between the cedar shingles. Through the windows, Laurel saw only rolling flames. She dashed to the tack room for a horsehair-filled cover and threw it over her head and shoulders for protection. She wrenched open the front door. Flames billowed from the house, fed by the rush of fresh air. The roar increased.

'Jimmy! Jimmy! Jason! Can you hear me? Are you in there?'

Only the roar of the infernal flame.

'Oh God! Save my children. Save my boys. Dear God. My God!' Even wrapped in the horse cover, Laurel could not fight her way into the burning house. She choked on the smoke. Flames licked at her hands. The roar of the fire got louder. Sparks flew as the rafters collapsed into the maelstrom. Laurel howled at the fire. She screamed at God. She sank slowly to her knees, not trying to escape the sparks that burned pinholes in the horse cover and singed her hair and face. Tears welled in her eyes and coursed down her cheeks. Their home was on the Paradise; now it was Laurel's Hell.

She curled into a foetal ball and screamed and screamed until her throat was cracked and bleeding. Jimmy, poor Jimmy. Five and so grown-up. Helpful. Thoughtful. Poor Jimmy. Gone to God. Laurel could only pray that he'd died before the hideous flames made a cinder of his small body. Jason. First born at Paradise. At three, his baby warblings were finally turning into coherent speech. He loved big brother Jimmy. Followed him everywhere. Wanted to do all that Jimmy could do. Gone. Burned in a blaze of pine-fed fire.

By morning, only the log walls and the stone chimney stood. Small flickers of flame played along the smoking logs. Laurel couldn't move. She dared not try to look among the ashes inside the gutted house. She sat with the horse cover around her shoulders. Sat and rocked back and forth and keened her pain to the heavens.

The first wagon arrived at mid morning. Seth Owens, the Bakers' nearest neighbor, drove the wagon with his wife Priscilla clinging grimly to the seat. She scrambled down almost before the wagon stopped and ran to Laurel.

'Laurel, oh Laurel. What on earth happened. Oh, your lovely home.'

'God damn the house,' Laurel screamed. 'God damn it. My boys. My Jimmy. My Jason. . . .' She could say no more, merely point at the ruins in speechless pain.

Priscilla gathered Laurel into her ample arms. 'Poor lass. Poor lass,' she crooned. Above Laurel's head she looked meaningfully at her husband and motioned with her head that he should look into the smoking ruins. 'Poor lass,' she crooned.

Laurel made no sound, but tears flooded from her eyes and cascaded down her singed face. She laid her head on Priscilla's shoulder and sobbed and sobbed.

Seth came back from the house. 'They're both in what's left of their beds, Laurel,' he said. 'I'm sure the smoke smothered them before the fire ever

9

reached the loft. Thank God for that. Still, you'll not be wanting to look at them, lass. Best to remember them as they were when you last saw them. I'll make some boxes for their burial.'

Laurel sat with her head on Priscilla's shoulder for a long time. 'It's all my fault,' she said in a tiny voice.

'That's crazy. Of course it's not your fault.'

'It is. I put them to bed and left them alone while I went out to meet Jack on the road back from Ponderosa. I banked the Franklin, but must have left the lamp burning on the table. I don't know what knocked it off, but that's what must have happened. I left them alone. If I'd stayed where I belonged, my boys would be alive.'

'Now, now, don't blame yourself. God works in mysterious ways. Now he's called your boys home. They feel no pain. And now they're singing with the angels.' Priscilla did her best to comfort Laurel, but couldn't reach her.

Laurel felt herself sinking into a deep dark place where she could neither think nor feel. She lost contact. Her awareness weakened. She felt the fires of Hell coming nearer and nearer. In her heart, she screamed and screamed, but made no sound. Only the tears and the pain seemed real. Still, she struggled from Priscilla's embrace, stood up, and looked at the smoking remains of her Paradise. Inside, she felt numb. Outside, she shivered.

'Let go,' she said to Priscilla. 'Let me go.' She shed the horse cover, wincing as her burned hands grasped the rough canvas. She stood on uncertain legs, almost unfeeling from remaining in the same position for so long. She took a step toward the house.

'Honey, don't,' Priscilla pleaded, reaching out to grasp Laurel's arm.

Laurel shrugged out of Priscilla's grasp. She could think only of seeing her sons, of bidding them farewell. She took another step toward the ruins, and another.

'Seth,' Priscilla called. 'Seth. She's going in.'

Laurel was dimly aware of running footsteps, but they seemed far away. She was already through the doorframe, and her thick boot soles crunched on ashes and embers. Her grieving self was a tiny hard ball in the pit of her stomach. Her empty eyes registered only what they saw and the sight failed to reach her heart. The loft had fallen with the rafters, but the fire had not consumed it. The little bodies still lay in their bunks, scraps of burnt bedclothes covering them. The heat had pealed off the skin but mercifully had not burned away their eyelids. In the aftermath of the blaze, they seemed to be still asleep; horribly burned, but sleeping.

'Come away, Laurel. Let them rest in peace. Let me take care of them for you.' Seth Owens touched her arm.

The emptiness deepened. From the depths of her despair, she could hardly hear Seth's voice. She let him lead her from the death chamber, once again to be enfolded in Priscilla's arms.

A spark lit the darkness. Jack would soon be home.

Jack would know what to do. Jack. Laurel leaned into Priscilla's embrace and waited for her husband to come home.

Seth Owens built two small boxes with pine boards and tools he found in the barn. He wrapped the two boys in saddle blankets, placed them in the boxes, and sealed the lids with horseshoe nails. He put the little coffins in an open stable until Laurel and Jack decided where their burial ground should be.

'Shall we clean up around, Laurel?' Seth asked.

Laurel heard the question from the bottom of the dark pit in her mind. She shook her head. 'Wait,' she said. 'Wait for Jack.'

Seth nodded.

Laurel took a deep breath. She couldn't just sit here. Things waited to be done. She staggered toward the granary with Priscilla a step behind.

'Laurel, honey, what are you doing?'

'Chickens need feed.' Laurel scooped a measure of oats from the bin with the usual bucket.

'Chick chick chick chick,' she called and broadcast the oats for the chickens to eat. No use milking the cows. The milk bucket probably burned with the house. She turned the calves in with the milk cows. They'd get an extra portion today. She sighed. When would Jack get home?

The second wagon came shortly after noon, and it came at a run. Frank Wills shouted at the team and slapped at their rumps with the ends of the reins, trying to urge them into yet greater speed. They came to a stop in a cloud of dust that drifted over the remains of the Paradise ranch house. 'Jeez,' he said to Seth. 'What happened here?

'Dunno yet. Laurel thinks it may have been a wayward lantern.'

Frank tested the air with a high thin nose. 'Does smell a bit like coal oil.'

Seth looked up, then tested the air himself. 'Does at that.'

'That's not why I'm here. We found Jack Baker's wagon at the bottom of Paradise Gorge. Where's Missus Baker?'

Seth motioned toward the granary. Laurel hurried across the yard. 'Frank Wills,' she called. 'Have you seen Jack?'

'I know this is hard, Missus Baker, your house burned down and all, but Jack's wagon is at the bottom of Paradise Gorge. Looks like something spooked the team and they went right off the edge, wagon and all. Nothing moving. Both horses dead. Some fellers climbing down there right now to see about Jack.'

The thunder of hoofs came before Laurel could speak. Two men Laurel knew only by sight reined their lathered mounts in beside Wills's wagon. 'We found Jack Baker,' one said. 'Neck broke. They're hauling him out of the gorge now.'

Laurel sank to her knees. The black pit threatened to consume her. First Jimmy and Jason. Now Jack. *Cut,* her mind said. *Bleed. Get out of this place where you can't think or even feel.* She fumbled in her trouser pocket for the clasp knife she always carried when

13

riding. Opening the blade, she slashed first her left arm, then her right. Pain. Blood. Then she cut her face from the hairline by her ear down to the point of her jaw. *I'm alive,* she thought. *Maybe the pain will take away the emptiness.* Bleeding profusely, she hacked away her long brown hair, sawing off each handful with the knife.

Men from Ponderosa brought Jack Baker to Paradise in the bed of a freight wagon. Laurel forced herself to look at her dead husband. The men had straightened out his arms and legs and he lay as if sleeping, his eyes closed, but his face smashed and gory from contact with the malpais of Paradise Gorge. Laurel knew he must be washed. She brought a bucket of water from the house spring, wet the bandana she'd worn about her neck when riding to look for him the night before, and used it to swab away the crusted blood from Jack's face.

'Let us do for him, Laurel,' said Seth Owens. 'We'll make a good box to hold his body until the resurrection. Just you leave him to us.'

Priscilla took Laurel away and enfolded her in strong arms and ample bosom. 'Now lass, now lass,' she crooned.

Laurel shrugged her off. Deep down in the black place that was her soul, she knew she must bid her family goodbye.

'Seth,' she called. 'Bury my men on the high ground behind the house. They always did like a clear view of Paradise Valley.' Then she collapsed into a heap in the front yard. She wasn't aware of the men digging holes in the place she'd indicated. She didn't see the two small boxes and one large box lowered into the graves and covered reverently with the spoil from the digging, and she didn't watch as they pounded the headboards into the loam at the heads of the graves. The neighbours burned Jack and the boys' names on the headboards with running irons from the tack room, along with 'Rest in Peace, 24 August 1880.'

CHAPTER 2

Doc Huntly larded and bandaged Laurel's burned forearms and hands. They were reddened but the skin was still intact. He decided the pinprick burns on her face from sparks and ashes could be left alone. He prescribed a dose of laudanum so she would sleep, but when she awoke, the dark bottomless pit inside her remained.

Gone. Gone. Those she loved. Those she cherished. Gone. When she closed her eyes, visions of her horribly burned sons and bashed and battered husband rolled across her eyelids. When she opened them, her eyes refused to focus. She groaned in pain.

'Are you awake, my dear?'

Laurel struggled to see who was speaking.

'Come, come. It's time to wake up. Time to have some breakfast.'

'Not hungry,' Laurel said, the words thick in her mouth.

'Oh but you must eat. Miss Swenson prepared gruel especially for your tender stomach. And if you don't eat, how do you expect to regain your strength?'

The voice was kindly but Laurel failed to catch the meaning.

'Gruel?' Still the word felt thick. Her tongue felt old and unused.

'Yes. Yes. Gruel. Good, hot gruel.'

Laurel peered at the speaker, opening her eyes wide, then making slits of them. The speaker blurred in her sight. It seemed to be a man. Light flashed off something. Eyeglasses? 'Gruel,' Laurel stated with her thick tongue. 'Not hungry.'

'Missus Baker. It is important that you wake up and eat. You need to shake off the laudanum and get something in your stomach to counteract the drug. Here, I will help you sit up so you can eat.'

'Who are you?' Laurel asked. 'Why this?' She struggled with the words. 'Sleep. Tired. Not hungry.'

Strong hands raised her to a sitting position and stuffed pillows behind her back. Bright light came in the window. She closed her eyes only to see her dead sons and husband tattooed on her eyelids. She opened them again and struggled to focus. The man's shape was not as fuzzy. His spectacles glinted light sometimes and he seemed to be smiling. 'That's better, Missus Baker. Now, Miss Swenson, our nurse, will feed you.'

Laurel felt something warm against her lower lip. In reflex, she opened her mouth a bit. A spoon slid in and dumped warm goo into her mouth. She smacked at the gruel and eventually it rolled down her throat. Then, suddenly she felt hunger rise from her stomach to her mouth and make it open again. Another spoonful of gruel. And another. Her sight cleared some. She could see the curtains at the window and make out the faces of the man and woman who watched her with concerned eyes. She ate all the gruel.

'Where am I and who are you?' she managed to say.

'I am Doctor Huntly. This is nurse Swenson. You are in my house in Ponderosa. Seth and Priscilla Owens brought you in for treatment of your burns and cuts and trauma.'

'Oh.' The food seemed to provide energy to clear Laurel's senses. The black pit remained at the centre of her being, but she at last was able to function. 'Can I go now?'

'Your hands and forearms suffered burns and I had to put stitches into the wounds on your arms and face. I would prefer you to stay two or three days.'

'I need to leave.' She couldn't force herself to say 'go home'. Paradise had burned. No one lived at Paradise any more. Yet she needed to be there.

'I certainly can't force you to stay, though I advise it. At least for another day.'

'Where are my clothes?'

'I sent them to the Chinaman's to be laundered. They should be back later today. Until then, why don't you rest?'

Rest. Laurel's body cried out for sleep, even though she'd eaten the gruel. 'I'll lie down then,' she said, struggling to get the pillows out from behind her. The nurse hurried over to pull the pillows out, leaving one for Laurel's head. She was asleep almost the moment her head touched the pillow. She didn't feel the nurse pull the bedclothes over her and quietly leave the room, and she didn't see the doctor look at her for another long moment, then stride from the room shaking his head.

Laurel awoke with the insides of her mouth so dry the skin felt as if it would crack. But now her sight was clear, as was her brain, though her headache made her cringe. The images of her sons and husband still burned on the insides of her eyelids, but she suspected that would always be so. Her clothing lay folded neatly on a chair, small clothes on top. Suddenly she realized she was naked beneath the nightgown. Who had stripped her? Who had seen her naked? Not that it mattered. She was just a tired old widow with no one left to fill her life. Tears welled and trickled down her burn-speckled cheeks, jagging in their downward track when they reached the bandage covering the slash that marred the left side of her face.

Nurse Swenson bustled into the room. 'Good day, missus. Are you feeling better now?'

'Somewhat. My head's splitting and my throat's terribly dry.' Laurel felt like talking would turn her throat bloody.

'Just a moment. I'll get you some water. Would you like some willow bark tea? It does marvels for headaches.'

'Yes please. And . . .'

19

The nurse turned, waiting for Laurel to continue.

'. . . and I'd like to get dressed.'

'Of course you may. That's why your clothing is close at hand. If you need to use the chamber pot, it's beneath the bed.'

Laurel's body was so dry she felt as if she'd not urinate for a month, but she nodded to show she understood what the nurse said.

'I'll get some water and tea for you, then,' Nurse Swenson said. She bustled from the room, and Laurel could hear her clanking about somewhere in the back of the house.

Laurel pushed herself into a seated position with her legs hanging over the side of the bed. Gingerly, favouring her sore arms and hands, she fished her pantaloons from the pile of laundry and thrust first her left then her right foot into the legs. She stood off the bed and onto the floor, straightening and pulling the pantaloons into place at the same time. She doffed the nightgown. Her laundered work shirt, which was originally one of Jack's, followed a light undershirt. She tucked both into the jeans, again castoffs of Jack's, which she wore when riding. She'd knitted the wool socks herself, using a small, tight weave. They felt good on her feet. If only her head would stop hurting; if only she could use her hands more freely.

The nurse returned with two cups, one of water and one of a dark brown tea brewed from willow bark. 'Drink the tea first,' she said, and placed the two cups on a sideboard by the bed. 'Call if you need me.'

'Could you tell me where my boots are?'

'My goodness. Why in the world would you need boots?'

'I'd like to know. Please.'

The nurse waved at the closet. 'In there.' She bustled from the room.

Laurel drank the tea in great gulping swallows. She wanted the headache gone. Then she sipped at the water, sloshing it around inside her mouth to help get rid of the dryness. Soon the banging in her skull became a dull throb and she began to think straight again.

The dark pit in her stomach stayed along with the images behind her eyelids. But more than anything else, Laurel wanted to be in Paradise. She found her boots and, wincing as her burned fingers went through the loops, pulled them on. Her coat and hat were in the same closet, along with the Yellow Boy Winchester she'd carried that night. She shrugged into the coat and let the hat hang down her back on its thong. With bandaged hands, she checked the action of the Winchester. The bullet she'd jacked into the chamber before was still there. She ejected it, closed the action without loading another cartridge, and shoved the ejected shell back into the magazine. She found the burns on her hands and fingers did not prevent her from operating the Winchester. She sighed.

'Miss Swenson,' she called. Her voice regained some of its normal strength.

'Coming.' The nurse burst through the door as if

there were some kind of emergency and came to a sudden stop when she saw Laurel in coat and hat with a rifle on the bed. 'Oh. Goodness.' Her hands went to her cheeks.

'I'd like to speak with Doctor Huntly.'

'Oh, goodness, he's making a house call. He'll be back shortly, I'm sure. Won't you just relax and wait? It shouldn't be long,' the nurse said, and almost ran from the room.

Nurse Swenson came with a dinner of beef and beans and coarse johnnycake. 'Please eat,' she said. 'Surely the doctor will return soon.'

Laurel ate, and found herself hungry despite the dark pit of blackness in the centre of her being. Her hunger was satisfied, however, long before the food was gone. Laurel left a goodly portion on the plate. The blackness inside remained.

Doc Huntly returned just after the nurse had taken away the remains of Laurel's dinner. She'd clucked at the portion left uneaten. 'What's the matter, Missus Baker?' he asked, entering the room after talking with Nurse Swenson.

'I'm ready to leave, Doc. My headache is gone. My arms feel sore but all right. There's no reason why I should stay. How much do I owe you?' Laurel's face looked made of stone.

'Hmmm. Yes. Well, we can't make you stay here. Have you somewhere to go?'

'I'll go to Paradise.'

'How?'

'How did I get here?'

22

'I gather the Owenses brought you in their wagon.'

'They brought my rifle. Chances are they brought Angel, too.'

'Angel?'

'My horse. I'll go to the livery stable and see.' Laurel buttoned her coat and reached for her rifle. 'If you'll excuse me,' she said.

The doctor stood aside.

Laurel turned back. 'How much do I owe you, Doctor?'

'I reckon two bucks would do it.'

'I'll bring the money when I come in next. Is that all right?'

'Of course.'

'Thanks. I'll be leaving then. If Angel's not at the livery, I'll borrow one of their nags.'

The livery stable stood just two blocks from Doc Huntly's place, but to Laurel it felt like two miles. The short walk pulled at her hamstrings and made her heart pound. Just scorched arms and burned hands with a few specks of burn on her face, oh, and three deep slashes; why does losing those you love suck away so much physical strength?

'Lew,' she called from the gate. 'Lew! You in there?'

'Coming, damn it, coming! You don't have to yell your head off . . . oh, 'scuse me, Missus Baker. What's going on?' Lew Jensen's bald head wore a fringe of curly white hair and his grey walrus moustache was stained yellow by his favorite Mail Pouch chewing tobacco.

'Is Angel here, Lew?'

'Nope.'

'You got a plug I can ride to Paradise?'

'Plug? Whose horses are you calling plugs?' Lew swelled up like a horned toad.

Ordinarily, Laurel would have laughed. Now, she didn't have the strength. 'Just give me a nice gentle horse that can make it to Paradise,' she said in a tired voice.

'You OK, Missus, face and hands all bandaged up like that?'

'I can make it, Lew. Just get me a horse and saddle.'

'It'll cost a dollar.'

'Lew, I just come from Doc Huntly's. I don't have a dollar on me, but you know I'm good for it. I'll bring your dollar back with the horse as soon as I can. Good enough?' Laurel clung to the gatepost and locked her knees to keep from collapsing.

Lew gave her a long searching look. 'You can ride the black mare with four white stockings,' he said. 'She's gentle as your own mother's bosom. I'll get her saddled up. You just sit down on that bench over there and wait.'

Laurel dragged herself to the bench against the wall of the stable and sat down with a grateful sigh. She laid the rifle in her lap and leaned back against the wall. She closed her eyes for a moment and awoke when Lew Jensen shook her shoulder.

'Missus,' he said. 'Are you up to riding all the way to Paradise?'

'I can ride, old man. Come on, help me into the saddle.' She stood with visible effort and walked to the offside of the mare. 'I'll need a scabbard for this rifle,' she said.

Lew got an old scarred scabbard and inserted it beneath the stirrup leathers and tied it to the skirts. 'That do?' he asked.

'Fine,' Laurel said, shoving the Yellow Boy into the scabbard. She went back to the onside and stood by the stirrup. 'Got a mounting block?'

'No. I'll just give you a boost.' He laced his hands together and leaned down so Laurel could get her left boot into the palms of his hands as if she were stepping into a stirrup. 'Ready?' he asked.

'Ready,' she said.

Lew lifted as she straightened up and threw her right leg over the cantle. He continued lifting until she was firmly in the saddle.

She sighed and slipped her boots into the stirrups. 'A little short,' she said, 'But they'll do. See you in a few days, Lew. Thanks a bundle.'

Lew gave her a wave and went back into the stable. Laurel clucked at the black mare and set out for the Alpine mail road at a gentle walk. 'You've got a lovely gait,' Laurel told the horse. 'You just keep it up and I'll sleep while we go along.'

She dozed as the gentle mare clip-clopped her way east along the mail road, but was awake enough to rein the black onto the wagon track to Paradise. She arrived after dark. The smell of smoke was still in the air, along with the acrid scent of coal oil. After undoing the girth, she pulled the saddle off the mare, removed the bridle, and turned her into the paddock.

With a saddle for a pillow and a saddle blanket as a ground cloth, Laurel slept until well into the morning. In fact, it was the sound of horses' hoofs on the hard ground that woke her. She jammed on her floppy hat and pulled the Winchester from the old scabbard. Three horses lined up in front of the burned-out house. Laurel stepped out of the tack room and jacked a cartridge into the chamber of the Yellow Boy. 'Nice of you to come visiting,' she said, holding the Winchester casually pointing at a space between the riders.

'Boss?' said one, his hand a claw over the ivory handle of an Army Colt.

'Easy, Rawlins. Let me take care of this.' The man addressed as 'boss' touched his hat in salute to Laurel. 'We were not aware you were on the premises,' he said. His voice was cultured and his clothing spoke of money – striped California pants over shiny Wellington boots, a vest brocaded black on grey, an off-white linen shirt, and a pearl grey frock coat with a dark grey ascot at his throat. 'My name is Robert Dunn,' he said. 'I work with Fletcher Comstock, and these men work with me. We heard of the tragedy at Paradise ranch and came to see for ourselves.'

'There's nothing to see.'

'Missus Baker. One woman can never make a go of a ranch this size. Especially not now, with your hands and face injured. I'm willing to make you a fair offer for your land.'

Laurel moved the Yellow Boy so it was pointing directly at Robert Dunn's belly. 'Paradise is mine,' she said. 'And I don't like uninvited guests.' The man called Rawlins still held his hand clawed over his sixgun. 'Just in case you get any ideas, Mr Rawlins,' she said, 'you can't draw a Colt fast enough to keep me from killing your boss, even with bandages on my hands. Now, would you three gentlemen leave me to my losses and my ranch. Please.'

Dunn tipped his hat. 'Sorry to catch you in such a foul mood, Missus Baker. We'll be back another day.'

Laurel kept the rifle on Dunn as the three men rode away, and walked away from the tack room to watch them out of sight. Something about Robert Dunn didn't sit right.

CHAPTER THREE

Laurel stood in place for a long time after the three men moved out of sight. Then she let the hammer of the rifle down. She'd keep it close to hand and she'd keep a cartridge in the chamber, but there were chores to be done and a place to clean up. She leaned the rifle against the tack room wall.

One of the things Laurel liked most about her Paradise ranch was its springhouse. Jack built it even before he started work on the ranch house. The little house was made of stone and hardly tall enough to stand up in. Rock slabs formed a square pool with shelves for cream crocks and milk jugs. Paradise Creek itself began as a spring about nine thousand feet above sea level in the mountains to the south-east.

After the springhouse, Jack dug a root cellar. At the moment it stored only a few carrots, but Laurel would have to get the root crops out of the ground soon or the deep frosts would come and ruin them.

Laurel had given birth to two children in wikiups

with the help of an Apache medicine woman: one near Dos Cabezas mountains where she and Jack prospected for gold to buy land, one here at Paradise when the springhouse and the horse paddocks were all they had. Laurel reckoned she could make do again if she had to. Domestic animals, however, can't take care of themselves when they're corralled. Now that Dunn and his gunmen were gone, Laurel started on her chores.

She turned the two Jersey milk cows out to pasture. They'd not go far from their nightly bait of oats. She left the calves with them for now. Angel stood patiently in his stall so Laurel fed him oats then put him in the paddock with the livery mare. She'd fork out the droppings later.

Seth Owens came in mid morning, a big horse trotting along behind his wagon. 'Heard you'd left Ponderosa,' he said. 'You gonna take care of Rafter P on your own?'

'I am. Jack's here. Up on the hill with Jimmy and Jason. They'll watch over me,' Laurel said, with a tremble in her voice and resolve in her eyes.

'Your team went to the bottom of Paradise Gorge,' Seth said, 'so I brung you one of our work horses. She's tough and not too big for you to handle, I reckon. You'll be wanting to plough the potatoes out of the ground afore long.'

'Thanks, Seth. I was figuring on using a shovel. Now I can do it the easy way.'

'You gonna be OK here?'

'The Rafter P is my place. Jack and the boys wouldn't

want me going anywhere else. I'll make out.' Even as she said the words, the blackness at the pit of her being threatened to break out and scream at the futility of it all. What was left, after all, with those she loved lying buried on the hill, what was left? Why go on? Why play at being strong? 'I'll make out,' she said again.

'You OK with those hands?' Seth asked. 'I can help a bit if you need any. What say?'

Laurel bowed her head, then looked up. 'I'll make out,' she said through clenched teeth. With great effort, she smiled. 'Thanks for your generosity, Seth. Tell Priscilla I'm doing all right.'

'Just being neighbourly,' Seth said. He climbed down from the wagon seat, untied the work mare, and handed the lead rope to Laurel. 'Her name is Molly and she's plumb gentle. She knows how to pull and she does what she's told.'

Laurel took the lead rope.

Seth clambered back up on his wagon seat. 'Good luck, girl,' he said, clucked to the team and made his way back up the wagon track toward the Owens homestead.

Laurel leaned against Molly the mare. 'There'll be a day when we'll have to work our fingers to the bone,' she said, 'but right now you just graze in the paddock with Angel and the livery horse, OK?'

Molly didn't answer, but she made no protest when Laurel led her through the gate to the paddock.

The rattle of Seth's wagon faded into the distance,

and the Rafter P ranch on Paradise was quiet once more. The darkness settled into the pit of Laurel's stomach. She had to talk with Jack.

The mountain dogwoods down by Paradise Creek shed their flowers in May. In early fall there were no blossoms to put on Jack's and the boys' graves, so Laurel smoothed the mounds of earth on the graves and sat down on the grass beside Jack's grave marker.

'I can't stay long, honey,' she said. 'There's lots of things that need doing with you not here. The garden needs hoeing and the tomatoes need picking. The little apple trees we set out last year have half a dozen apples on them. I could bake you an apple pie if you were just here . . . and if our house weren't burned down.' A tear escaped the corner of her eye and trickled over the burn pits on her face. 'There's squash and peas and string beans and pinto beans and corn in the field. I don't know if the Franklin is usable. I haven't even started to clean up the house yet. Oh, Jack. It's so lonely without you here. So lonely. Yet this Paradise and the Rafter P is what we dreamed of, and I won't let that dream die. I won't. I can't.' She lowered her face to her knees and sobbed.

Angel whinnied in the paddock. Laurel's head came up. Her eyes went first to the wagon track from Ponderosa. Nothing. She looked at Angel. The steel-dust stood stock still, his ears pricked toward the pines to the south.

Laurel leaped up and ran down the hill to the tack room. Her breath coming in great gulps, she grabbed up the Winchester from where she'd left it leaning against the wall. Ignoring the pain in her hands, she thumbed the hammer back and turned to face in the same direction as Angel. Apaches appeared at the edge of the wagon track. One moment Laurel saw nothing, the next four braves and a woman stood not fifty feet away.

A shaft of ice travelled up Laurel's spine. These were not the Chiracahua Apaches she knew. Not Alchesay. Not the medicine woman. Still, one of the men held his right hand up, palm out, fingers splayed. No weapon. They came in peace. Laurel uncocked the hammer of the Winchester and let the muzzle point at the ground.

The Apaches advanced. When they stood only a few feet away, the leader, the man who had held up his hand, spoke. 'I am called P'tone,' he said. 'We live here in the White Mountains. Our cousins from the mountains called Dragoons asked us to visit you. We see you lost your home, your man, your sons. We see your burned home. Where are your men?'

Laurel pointed at the graves.

The Apache nodded. 'It is good to be on a high place,' he said. 'Tonight, when the moon appears, we will do a spirit dance for your men. First we eat.'

One of the men carried a haunch of venison over his shoulder. Laurel showed him were to hang it in the root cellar. The woman had a pouch of bleached acorn meal, wild onions, and sego lily roots. 'Soon we eat,' she said, and Laurel realized she'd had nothing to eat all day.

'What can I do?'

'You wait. We cook,' the woman said.

Laurel returned to the seat by the tack room and sat with the rifle in her lap. The Apaches made a small fire on the flat in front of the burned and blackened house. Soon venison was roasting on sticks, seasoned lightly with salt. A bark container held the wild vegetables and small pieces of meat. It sat on a rock in the midst of the fire, the water inside keeping it from burning. The woman mixed acorn flour with water and salt, patted the dough into palm-sized patties, and roasted them on a flat rock tilted to face the fire.

When the food was ready, Laurel and the Indians sat cross-legged around the fire to eat venison skewered on sticks and roasted, stewed vegetables from cups the woman had found in the burned-out cabin, and baked acorn cakes with their hands. Laurel found the food wholesome and filling, and she feared she ate more than her share. 'Thank you so much,' she said to the woman, handing her the empty cup.

'You eat more?'

'The food was delicious, but I couldn't eat more. Why are you doing this for me?'

'Our cousins the Chiracahua say you and your husband, you and your sons, are good people. Never steal. Never hurt. Never lie. Always have coffee. Never turn any hungry Apache away. We help.'

They sat, comfortable with each other, until the moon rose and moved high into the sky. The four men left for a while and came back dressed for the spirit dance, one man for each of the cardinal directions. Tiny bells jingled with every step. Black hoods covered their heads, with great slatted crowns attached. Mostly their clothing was buckskin, cleverly decorated with beads and porcupine quills. One wore no shirt and his torso was covered with large white dots.

The woman produced a flat drum and a stick ringed with bells. She handed the bell stick to Laurel. 'Come,' she said, and led the way to the graves of Laurel's three men.

The woman started a throbbing rhythm on the drum and indicated that Laurel was to shake the bells in time with the beat, which she did. The woman sang and the four spirit men danced. To Laurel it sounded like the woman was singing '*nayo nayo nayo hohowana han na, nayo nayo nayo*' but not understanding more than a few words of Apache, Laurel had no idea what the words meant. The men danced in a large circle around the graves. Laurel shook her bell stick. The Apache woman beat her throbbing drum and sang. The ceremony went on and on and on, coming to an end only when the moon dipped below the tops of the pines.

The men disappeared. The woman put away the drum and the bells. 'The spirits will rest now,' she said. 'When you need help, we are nearby. Send a smoke. We will see.'

'Thank you,' Laurel said. The darkness at the pit of her soul seemed not as leaden and heavy as before. 'Thank you. And tell P'tone thank you as well. May I ask your name?'

The woman bowed her head and stared at the ground for a long moment. Then she lifted her head and looked into Laurel's eyes. 'My parents named me Elina. They wished for me to grow up bright and clever.'

'Elina. I will not forget. I am Laurel. A tree that never loses its leaves.'

'I too will remember. Laurel. I like the sound.'

The man named P'tone appeared at the edge of the pines on the hill. He motioned for Elina to come. She picked up her pack of implements. 'Be well, Laurel,' she said.

'And you, Elina,' Laurel replied.

In moments the Apaches were gone and the dawn lighted up the eastern skyline.

The spirit dance had lasted nearly all the night, but Laurel felt refreshed. She must think about something for breakfast. There would be bacon in the root cellar and eggs in the henhouse. Laurel found herself humming, and she could hear the words: *nayo nayo nayo ho howana nan na nayo nayo nayo.*

She got a pair of leather gloves from the tack room, picked up a hatchet, and strode into the burnt-out house. The Franklin stove stood against what was left of the south wall. Rafters had fallen across it, but a few blows from the hatchet cleared them away. Her cast-iron frying pans and Dutch ovens would be in the cabinet at the left-hand side of the stove. The top of the cabinet was burned through but the doors still stood. Laurel pulled at a loop handle and the door fell off into the layer of charcoal and ashes that covered the pounded-earth floor. All the cast-iron utensils sat as she had placed them, except the heat from the fire had caused them to burn through the shelving and settle to the bottom of the cabinet. She extracted a ten-inch frying pan. It would do for bacon and eggs, the proper way to start a morning on a ranch. She still hummed the spirit dance song.

She scoured the pan with sandy mud at the edge of Paradise Creek and rinsed it well. All the soot mixed with the mud and disappeared. With the same clasp knife she'd used to slash her arms and face, Laurel cut three thick strips of bacon. A short trip to the henhouse and she had two big brown eggs for her breakfast. No frybread or biscuits this morning, but that could soon be remedied. She hummed the spirit dance song as she built a fire in the same place the Apaches used last night. When the little fire was down to coals, Laurel sat the frying pan on it and put in the bacon, cut into inch-long pieces. Her mouth began to water.

She stirred the pieces of bacon with a stick stripped from a nearby aspen and trimmed for use. Gradually they turned golden brown and bacon grease collected in the bottom of the pan. Laurel cracked an egg on the edge of the pan, opened it and let the yolk and white spread into the pan. She did the same with the second egg, then stirred the mass of egg and bacon together until she had a golden mound of steaming food.

She rescued a big spoon from the burned house and wiped it clean with a piece of flour sack from the tack room. Frying pan in hand, she dug into the scrambled egg and bacon. The big pan was empty in minutes. Warmth filled Laurel's stomach and her smile stretched the stitched slash on her face. She felt the small beginnings of hope for the first time since Jack had died.

CHAPTER FOUR

Robert Dunn sat across the big desk from Fletcher Comstock, owner of the Comstock sawmill going up across Bog Creek from the town of Ponderosa. Comstock dammed Bog Creek at the edge of town, and the resulting log pond now had 300 acres under water.

'When the buzz saws start running, Bob, they'll eat Ponderosa logs at a rate of one log every five minutes, ten hours a day. You'll have to be dumping a hundred and twenty logs into that pond every day just to stay even.'

'We're planning on hauling a hundred fifty a day,' Dunn said. 'More than enough for your saws.'

'How long can you keep that up?'

'The wagon track to East Fork is through, and the 'jacks are cutting logs as we speak. Ready to haul by the first of the week.'

'Don't let me down, Bob. I need those logs. I already have orders for lumber and the country's growing fast.'

'You got it, Fletcher. First wagonload's in on Monday.'

'Good.' Fletcher Comstock turned away. The meeting was over.

Damn. Dunn jammed his hat on his head and left the office. *Damn.* While the wagon track to East Fork was indeed ready, the stands of Ponderosa pine were heavily interspersed with spruce and fir. Hundreds of stately pines marched up the sides of the White Mountain foothills, but it would be hell logging them out. Dunn stomped down the street toward Jimmy's Kitchen. At least he could have a good cup of coffee. Then he changed his mind. A new saloon had gone up in Bogtown, across the creek, and Dunn needed a drink. He collected his horse at the livery, paying a quarter for the stall and the oats, and rode up Main Street to Corduroy Road, took the downgrade to Bog Creek, splashed across the ford, and tied the bay gelding to the hitching rail in front of the new saloon. Old Glory, the sign said. A couple of shots of Turley's Mill would hit the spot. Dunn had some thinking to do. He always thought more clearly with a bottle of whiskey at his side.

'Evening,' the barkeep said. He wiped the bar in front of Dunn. 'What'll it be?'

'You got Turley's Mill?'

'Ten dollars a bottle, mister. No shots.'

'Gimme a bottle.' Dunn dug an eagle from his vest pocket and slapped it on the bar. 'And a clean glass.'

'Coming up.' The bartender reached under the

counter for a bottle of the good whiskey and took a glass from a pyramid stacked next to the bottles displayed before the bar mirror. 'One bottle of Turley's Mill, and our cleanest glass, especially for you, Mr—?'

'Dunn. Robert Dunn.'

'Jake Holladay,' the bartender said, 'but people call me Jinx. Shake hands with me and you're bound to lose at poker, so they say.'

Dunn half smiled. 'I'll stick to Turley's Mill, then. Costs less.' He took the bottle and glass to the back table and sat in the chair against the wall. A shot of Turley's Mill and he felt the warmth of good whiskey spreading through him. Two shots, and his worries began to shrink. Now he could begin planning.

He downed another shot.

Damn that Baker woman. She was supposed to give up when the ranch house burned. Damn.

Dunn poured a fourth shot and drank it down.

At least his men got it right when they spooked Baker's horses and wagon off the cliffs into Paradise Gorge. Baker didn't survive the fall; no one could. Dunn gave his shot glass a little smile.

That woman couldn't keep a ranch alive all by herself. A woman can't go long without a man. She'd be ready to sell within the week. Or maybe two. He'd get Dirk and Red to ride out to Paradise with him then. Make an offer. One she couldn't turn down. But if she did, well, there were other ways. He drank another shot.

A card game started two tables away. Two cowboys sat opposite each other. The dealer looked professional. A drummer took the fourth seat. Dunn glanced at the table, then ignored the game.

Dunn's lumberjacks stayed on the mountainside, camped just off East Fork. The wagons could haul six to ten twelve-foot logs each, depending on their girth. Dunn figured fifteen wagons a day. He'd lined up ten wagons and twenty teams of six Belgian draft horses each. With those good draft horses, he'd have no problem getting a hundred and fifty logs a day to the pond, give or take a few. Dunn smiled as he refilled the shot glass.

The problem was trees. Lots of trees on East Fork, but hard to get at and hard to get out. If he had the Paradise ranch, though, he could access Ponderosa pines with no problem. Paradise country wasn't high enough for spruce or fir to be a problem, and the mail road would make hauling easy. He needed that ranch. Dunn drank his glass of Turley's Mill. He'd give her a week, then make his offer. If that didn't work, he'd do whatever he had to do.

'Good evening.'

Dunn looked up. The speaker was overweight and wore sleeve garters over a white shirt with no collar. His ingratiating smile rubbed Dunn the wrong way. 'Do I know you?' he asked.

'I always like to greet gentlemen who patronize our establishment for the first time. My name is Bart Sims. I own Old Glory. We appreciate you coming in. I see you know good whiskey.'

'You charge a good price for it.'

'The good things in life come at a price.' Sims's smile

looked more like a smirk. 'Might I ask your name, sir?'

'Robert Dunn.'

Sims snapped his fingers at the barkeep. 'Jinx, bring another bottle of Turley's Mill for Mr Dunn. Compliments of the house.'

The bartender came over and handed the bottle to Sims, who put it carefully on Dunn's table next to the bottle he'd already half emptied. 'You don't need to pay for drinks in my saloon, Mr Dunn,' Sims said. 'May I sit at your table for a moment?'

Dunn nodded at a chair.

'Thank you.' Sims put his elbows on the table and leaned toward Dunn. 'Mr Dunn,' he said. 'Ponderosa is growing. Mr Comstock's sawmill will soon begin operations. Your logging operation has already, I believe, started cutting pines on East Fork.' He signalled to the bartender, who brought Sims a mug of beer.

'The army set up a camp called Kinishba on the plateau above White River,' the saloon owner said. 'Two companies of yellow legs. The soldiers from Camp Kinishba can entertain themselves right here at Old Glory, as can the sawyers and the lumberjacks along with the cowboys from the Bar B and Cooley's ranch at the Rincon.' Sims sipped at his beer. 'Certainly, when your men need a place to relax and refresh themselves, you will mention the delights of Old Glory.'

Sims took two gulping swallows of beer before facing Dunn again. 'Business often involves cooperation, Mr Dunn. You can cooperate with me, and I with you. At the moment, all I can do is see that you have what you wish to drink. Later, there may be other ways I can help.'

Dunn drank another shot of Turley's Mill. Damn but this man was long-winded. Still, free whiskey appealed to him. He refused to drink house whiskey – alcohol mixed with tobacco and chili peppers and rattlesnake heads – but he didn't like the ten-dollar-a-bottle price for the good stuff. 'I could mention Old Glory,' he said.

Sims smiled. 'That would be first rate, Mr Dunn. And as the town grows, I'm sure there will be other things I can do for you in addition to the Turley's Mill. Now, I must go watch the card game for a few moments. Every game here must be on the up-and-up. Excuse me, if you please.' Sims stood. 'Hope to be seeing more of you at Old Glory, Mr Dunn. And we welcome your lumberjacks and teamsters as well. He tipped his hat and stepped over to observe the card game.

Sims was right about Ponderosa growing. There was even some talk of hiring a marshal. The town had grown up on a flat north of Bog Creek. Fletcher Comstock and the other members of the Ponderosa Ring laid the streets out square and named them for local trees. The Alpine mail road looped around to become Main Street. Comstock built a hotel on Main and Jim Clark opened Jimmy's Kitchen. Houses went up on Oak Street and Ash Street and Walnut and Maple; or on the cross-streets of Pine, Spruce, and Fir. Corduroy Road, which linked Ponderosa with

Camp Kinishba and points west, intersected Main Street and had a downgrade that took it to the ford on Bog Creek. A small cluster of tarpaper shacks and drinkeries grew up across the creek, and became known as Bogtown. At the moment, Old Glory was Bogtown's largest structure. But the sawmill would bring workers and put money in their pockets. Many other businesses would flourish off the mill, and make yet more money. Old Glory would give the men a place to blow off steam. That meant girls would soon be coming. Dunn caught Sims's eye and waved him back to his table.

'Who's going to run the whorehouse?' he asked.

Sims smirked. 'New building going up just down the road, Mr Dunn. I understand Miss Alice Murdock plans for it to house her Institute for Wayward Young Women.'

'Where's she at?'

'At the moment, I believe she has a room at the Comstock Hotel. No boarding house in Ponderosa, you know. We're lucky to have Gardner's Mercantile.'

Dunn gulped a shot of Turley's Mill and stood. 'I'll be leaving,' he said. 'Just have Jinx keep my bottle under the counter. I'll be back.' He put a finger to the brim of his hat in farewell to Sims and walked carefully from the saloon.

At the Comstock Hotel, Dunn tied his bay to the hitching rail and strode into the lobby.

'Key, Mr Dunn?' The clerk asked.

Dunn held out his hand for the key. Then, leaning over the counter to be nearer the clerk's ear, he said,

44

'I understand Miss Alice Murdock has a room here. I'd like to know her room number.'

'Oh, Mr Dunn. I couldn't give out another guest's room number. Besides, Miss Murdock left for supper at Jimmy's Kitchen only a few minutes ago.'

'How would I recognize her?'

'Well, her face is quite freckled. Her teeth stick out just a little. She's got red hair the colour of a forest fire, all piled up on her head with little ringlets hanging over her ears. And she's wearing a yellow checked dress. I'm sure you won't mistake her for anyone else.'

Dunn grinned. 'Thank you.' He returned the key. 'I'll pick this up later.'

'Yessir, Mr Dunn.'

The night air and the ride up from Old Glory gave Dunn more equilibrium and he didn't have to walk so carefully. He strode next door to Jimmy's Kitchen to find Bucktooth Alice Murdock.

Like the hotel, Jimmy's Kitchen was made of lumber produced in trial runs at the Comstock mill. The exteriors were painted white, but the interiors smelled of new-cut pine. Blonde planking extended from floor to ceiling, and coal-oil lamps on the walls filled the restaurant with warm yellow light. Dunn swept his gaze across the customers. Fletcher Comstock sat alone at a corner table. Two men in flannel shirts and denim bibbed overalls ate their dinner at the centre table. The only woman in the house wore a yellow checked dress cut lower at the neckline than the ordinary housewife preferred, and her red hair picked up highlights from the lamps and almost sparkled. Dunn strode to her table and removed his hat. 'Miss Murdock,' he said. 'Would you allow me to sit with you at your table. My name is Robert Dunn.'

She looked up and smiled. While her front teeth protruded somewhat, her eyes were large and blue and framed with carefully applied kohl. Her cheeks looked slightly rouged, as were her lips. 'Of course, Mr Dunn. I much prefer conversation to eating alone. Please sit down.'

Jimmy's wife Madge came to get Dunn's order. 'Supper?' she asked. He nodded. 'Your choice of beef and beans or beef enchiladas.'

'Enchiladas,' Dunn said. 'Have you ordered, Miss Murdock?'

'I have. We seem to have similar tastes.'

Madge bustled back to the kitchen.

Alice Murdock cocked her head at Dunn. 'You've not come to my table by accident tonight, Mr Dunn. What do you have on your mind?'

Dunn plunged ahead. 'I understand you're start-ing a new institution down across Bog Creek,' he said.

Alice nodded.

'I'd like to give you a thousand dollars in gold,' Dunn said. 'What percentage of your new business would that buy me?'

Alice's eyes lit up. 'Why Mr Dunn. You must be an angel in disguise. I was in need of some ready cash. Your infusion of capital into Miss Murdock's Institute for Wayward Young Woman would purchase a one-fourth share, I would say.'

'Make that one-third and we have a deal,' Dunn said.

Alice's smile widened. 'Done,' she said. 'Pun intended.'

'I have a bottle of Turley's Mill in my room,' Dunn said. 'Perhaps after dinner we could seal our partnership with a drink of good whiskey in room 26 at the Comstock.'

'Why Mr Dunn. That invitation sounds delightful.' She ducked her head and looked at Dunn from beneath her dark eyebrows. 'And who knows what might happen.'

CHAPTER FIVE

Laurel saddled Angel early. The sun had not yet topped the mountains to the east and dew covered the grass of Paradise Valley. The creek seemed to steam in the early morning, and a few mule deer watered from the far side. One day soon, she'd have to kill one of the deer. Better one of them than one of her precious cows. She still wore her flannel shirt and Jack's old Levi's. She'd washed them in creek water and soused the dirt out with laundry soap made from pig fat and lye. Luckily, the laundry tub and the washboard had survived the fire. Laurel retrieved twenty dollars from their ranch-building fund in a clay pot buried in the corner of the barn, mounted the steeldust gelding, pulled her floppy hat low, and turned Angel toward Ponderosa with the livery horse in tow.

The wagon track took the high ground south of Paradise Creek before running into the mail road as it climbed up onto the malpai plateau that bordered Paradise Gorge. Laurel walked Angel up the wagon track, taking time to look over her ranch. The parcel she and Jack had purchased from Don Alfredo comprised ten sections of land. Its borders began where Paradise Creek tumbled into the eastern end of the valley, and ended where the creek ducked into the mouth of Paradise Gorge just over five miles away. Not a large spread. Just over six thousand acres, and some of that in timber on the southeast corner. Ample water from Paradise Creek made the ranch more than enough to raise a family . . . except Laurel no longer had a family.

She brushed away a strand of brownish hair and ignored the tear that trickled down her scared face. She and Jack had a dream; a dream of independence on a high mountain ranch; a dream of fat white-faced cattle and fleet, strong horses; a dream of children on the land where they could run and play and learn to work; a dream of freedom. She made a new vow. She'd pursue that dream, as long as she could ride a horse and walk behind a plough.

Angel knew the way to Ponderosa and trotted along with minimum direction from Laurel. He stopped at the livery stable of his own accord. Lew Jensen opened the gate. 'See you got my horse back in one piece,' he said.

'And fatter, too,' Laurel said. 'I should charge you for the oats.' She smiled. 'Here's the dollar I owe you, Lew. Thanks so much for the use of the mare.'

Lew took the dollar and scrutinized the mare. 'Don't see any damage,' he said. 'We're even. Come back any time you need a nag to ride.'

49

'Thought you didn't have any nags.'

Lew laughed. 'One or two, one or two.'

'Later, Lew. Thanks again.' Laurel reined Angel down Main Street, where she stopped in front of Doc Huntly's office. Dismounting, she tied Angel to the hitching rail and knocked on Doc Huntly's door. Miss Swensen opened it.

'Why Missus Baker. How are you today? My, but your bandages are dirty.'

'Ranching is a dirty business. Is the doc in?'

'He should be back in a few minutes. Would you like to wait?'

Laurel smiled. 'For a cup of your fine coffee, Miss Swensen, I'd wait forever.'

Miss Swensen dimpled. 'Come in, then. You can sit on the divan and I'll fetch you a cup of coffee.' She scurried from the room.

Laurel looked at the bandages on her hands and arms. She'd paid no attention to them while at Paradise. She did what she had to do, and if the bandages got wet or dirty, it was because she worked; she didn't sit around with her arms propped up on a table.

Laurel was on her second cup of coffee when Doctor Huntly returned.

'Ah, Missus Baker. Is something wrong?'

'It's been more than a week, doc, and I thought maybe you'd take the bandages off.'

'Could be. Could be. Let's have a look. Come on in to the surgery and we'll get those grubby things off your arms and face.' Doc Huntly led the way into a separate room.

Laurel didn't like the smell. She couldn't tell what the odours were, but they didn't seem healthy.

'Now. Let's have a look.' The doctor took a pair of scissors and snipped through the bandage on Laurel's right hand and arm. The burns were still red compared to her normal skin, and the sutured slash looked like a very large centipede. 'There's no need to bandage the burns any more,' he said. 'After, I'll give you some salve of olive oil and aloe vera. It's especially soothing to burned skin. Now, the sutures.'

Doc Huntly used a pair of sharp scissors to snip the stitches in Laurel's arms. He pulled the tread out with small pinchers. He then attended to the sutures in her face. 'There now,' he said. 'Those wounds have healed straight and thin. In a few months, you'll hardly be able to see them.'

'I appreciate all you've done, Doc. Here's the money I owe you.' She dug the dollars from her pocket and gave them to Doc Huntly. 'I hope I never have to see you again . . . in your official capacity, that is.'

'You're a fine patient, Missus Baker. You heal quickly and listen to most of my instructions. I too hope not to see you again, as a patient, that is. Here, let me get you some salve.'

Laurel took the small corked bottle of greenish salve. 'Goodbye, Doctor,' she said. 'I've got a lot to do, and not much time before frost to do it.'

Her next stop was Gardner's general store. She bought a canvas ground cloth, a wool Navajo rug, three blankets, and a box of cartridges for her Winchester carbine. On second thought, she also bought a box of rimfire .45 cartridges for the old Dragoon revolver Jack kept in the tack room. Saddle-bags full and blankets and rug rolled up inside the canvas and tied behind the cantle, Laurel mounted Angel and rode past the Comstock Hotel and Jimmy's Kitchen on her way toward the Alpine mail road.

'Missus Baker,' a voice called from the door to Jimmy's Kitchen. 'Missus Baker.'

Laurel reined Angel to a stop.

Robert Dunn stepped out of the door and onto the boardwalk that ran between the restaurant and the hotel. 'Missus Baker. I hope you are feeling better and have had a chance to think about your situation. I honestly will pay top dollar for your ranch. Top dollar.'

Laurel turned Angel and urged him to walk toward Dunn so that he had to step out of the way. 'Robert Dunn, my husband and my two sons lie buried on Rafter P land in Paradise Valley. They dreamed of good things for our ranch, and I aim to see their dreams come true. You can stack up double eagles all the way to the rafters, and I still won't sell you my land. Now excuse me. I must be getting back.'

'Let's go home, Angel,' she said to the horse, and he turned and started for the mail road, leaving Robert Dunn chewing his lip in frustration. She held tight to the saddle-horn so no one could see how her hands trembled.

*

Finn McBride liked the looks of the place. The small valley spread from the foot of the White Mountains out and across as far as Finn could see. Thousands of acres of choice grassland watered by a meandering creek that ran down the middle of the valley.

The man and his sons had been on the road since stopping at Saint Johns. Their wagon carried barbed wire, a little Giant Powder for clearing the way through rock, and the tools for building fences, but most ranchers preferred open range.

Finn examined the ranch buildings on high ground above the creek at the head of the valley. A holding pen and a paddock. A big barn with a tack lean-to attached. An outhouse and a spring house, one on the hill south of the buildings and the other a few steps away from the burned ruins of a ranch house. His eye also caught the headboards of the three graves on the hillside at the edge of the pines.

Horses in the paddock and milk cows near the creek told him the ranch was not abandoned, but no one greeted Finn's wagon. Sunset. Time to set up camp.

'Will, you unharness the mules down by that box alder tree. We'll camp there. Calvin, you can help by pulling out the Dutch ovens.' Finn took a .22 rifle from the wagon. 'I'll see if I can get something for supper,' he said.

Eight-year-old Will McBride had the same stubborn chin and shock of black hair as his father. He took the reins and, after his father climbed down with the rifle, he clucked to the two big mules. They obediently shambled toward the grove of box alders by the creek. He parked the wagon fifty feet back from the stream, set the brake, and climbed down to unharness the mules. 'You dig the fire pit, Cal,' he said.

'Ah, why do I have to do all the digging and scraping?'

' 'Cause you're big enough to do it and I got other chores.'

'Shit.'

Will cuffed Calvin on the ear. 'Don't use language like that, Calvin McBride. Mother taught us better.' Will and Cal's mother had died of the bloody flux a little more than two years ago, but Will still stuck to her rules.

Calvin mewled and sniffed. 'Quit picking on me. Just because you're eight and I'm six don't make you the boss of me.'

'When Pa's not here, it's up to me to see that you do what's right, Cal, and well you know it. Now dig the fire pit.'

Muttering under his breath, Cal started cutting turf with a shovel nearly twice his height. Off down the creek, the .22 spat. A few minutes later, it cracked again again. Then Finn McBride came walking back with two cottontail rabbits in hand. 'Good fire pit, son,' he said to Calvin. Finn saw signs of his Martha in the boy's light-brown hair and the sprinkle of freckles across his nose. 'Now, can you gather some wood for the fire? There'll be windfalls and such up in the trees across the wagon track. Use the hatchet, and take care.'

'Yes, Pa.' The six-year-old youngster shouldered the hatchet as if he had an important job to do, and set off for the pines across the wagon track.

'Want me to go with him, Pa?'

'He must learn to do things by himself, Will. There's little danger, I'm thinking. Here, skin these rabbits and dress them out. Throw the guts in the creek. Varmits and fish'll eat the leavings before morning.' He handed the rabbits to his son.

Finn deepened the fire pit somewhat and set out two cast-iron Dutch ovens, one small and deep, one shallow and wide. The sound of chopping came from back in the pines. A few minutes later, Calvin struggled to the fire pit with a fat pitchy-pine limb.

'Good lad,' Finn said. 'Will can take the axe to that while you go find us two more limbs just like it.' Calvin beamed and trotted back to the pine deadfall he'd found amongst the trees.

'When you get through with those cottontails, chop up that limb, Will, and get a fire going. You know where the lucifers are. Use only one, now.'

'I know, Pa,' Will said. He brought the skinned rabbits back to the fire pit and placed them in the wide Dutch oven, retrieved a double-bitted axe from the wagon, and soon had the pitch-pine limb chopped into a pile of wood suitable for a fire.

Finn pulled the grub box from the wagon. Then he measured out two cups of flour – he had two growing boys – for biscuits. He mixed the flour with

three pinches of salt and a quarter of a cup of salera-
tus soda, added creek water and stirred it with
Martha's big wooden spoon. When the ingredients
were thoroughly combined, Finn spread leftover
bacon grease around inside the wide Dutch oven and
used the spoon to scoop out gobs of dough, which he
put in the oven. He set the lid on the Dutch oven and
left the biscuits to rise while the fire burned down.

Will built a respectable fire, and Calvin came with
two more branches, which Will reduced to firewood.
Finn smiled. It was good to have two strong sons,
even with Martha gone. He dredged the pieces of
rabbit in flour and scooped a generous portion from
the lard bucket for the deep oven. He sat the oven at
the edge of the fire. The heat soon melted the lard,
but Finn waited until a tiny wisp of smoke rose from
the melted grease. Then he plopped in four pieces of
rabbit, which sizzled merrily and soon gave off a
tempting fragrance.

'Smells real good, Pa,' Will said. He squatted to
peer into the deep oven. 'Looks even better.'

'Move. I've got to turn the meat over,' Finn said,
shooing his son away. He turned the pieces of rabbit
with the wooden spoon. The hot lard left the flour
coating brown as fox fur. It popped and spit at the
new flesh, then settled down to fry the other side of
the rabbit pieces to the same golden brown.

'Time to put the biscuits on the fire,' Finn said. He
used the shovel to scrape together a layer of coals,
then set the wide Dutch oven on them. More coals
went on the Dutch oven lid so the biscuits would

bake top and bottom. Four pieces of rabbit were done. He put them on a tin plate from the chuck box and plopped the remaining pieces into the hot lard.

The biscuits soon baked and the pieces of rabbit fried. Finn pulled the Dutch ovens off the coals with a crook cut from a nearby box alder. 'Put more wood on the fire,' he said.

The pitch-pine soon caught and its merry flames gave off enough light to eat by.

'Plenty of meat, boys. Help yourselves.' Finn raked the coals and ashes off the biscuit oven and removed the lid. 'And lots of biscuits,' he said. But before he ate, Finn poured the hot lard back into the can. It would do to cook another day.

'The rabbit's right tasty, Pa,' Will said. 'Can I have another piece?'

'You can, boy, you surely can.'

The boys focused on meat and biscuits. Finn watched them with fondness in his eyes, then heard the sound of a horse moving through the night. He casually stood, walked to the wagon, and reached for the Winchester beneath the seat.

'Hello the fire.'

Finn walked back into the firelight, the Winchester held casually at his side. He realized the person who hailed the fire was a woman.

'Evening, ma'am,' he said.

She rode into the firelight on a steeldust gelding, a Yellow Boy Winchester across the saddlebows. 'I'm Laurel Baker,' she said, 'and you've set up camp on my land.'

CHAPTER SIX

'I'll be Finn McBeide,' the man said, 'and my sons are Willard and Calvin.' The boys were older than her Jimmy and Jason, but close enough to bring a catch to Laurel's throat.

'Ma'am. All we have is fried rabbit and biscuits,' McBride said, 'but you're welcome to sit and eat if you'd like.'

After a moment, Laurel shoved the Winchester into its scabbard and dismounted. She looped Angel's reins around the rim of the right-rear wagon wheel. 'All right,' she said. 'Women usually feed the men, so let's see how you are at feeding a woman.'

Finn grinned as he pulled an extra tin plate from the chuck box. 'Yes, ma'am. I'll let you be the judge.' He forked a rabbit quarter onto the plate and added a biscuit. 'The biscuits would be better sopped in some hot bacon grease, but they'll have to do.'

Laurel accepted the plate and squatted on her heels. She took the piece of rabbit by the leg bone and bit into the thigh. The meat was well done but

58

juicy and quite tender for wild game; just salty enough, and the flour dredging had turned into a crispy covering for the flavourful meat. She swallowed the bite of meat after chewing it well.

'If I ran a big cattle outfit,' she said, 'I'd hire you on as the old woman. The rabbit is really good.'

The boys were silent, eating rabbit and biscuits but keeping their eyes on Laurel from under the brims of their floppy hats. She alternated bites of rabbit with bites of biscuit until both were gone.

'You eat like it's been a while since you had food,' Finn said.

'Left Ponderosa before dinner,' Laurel said. 'First I've eaten since early morning.' She threw the bone and gristle of her rabbit quarter out onto the meadow grass. It'd be gone before the sun rose. She handed the empty plate back to Finn McBride. 'Thanks for the food,' she said.

'You're more than welcome,' Finn said. 'If you don't mind, we'll camp here tonight and be on our way in the morning.'

'Fine' Laurel replied. 'I know it would be nice to sit around the fire, have some hot coffee, and talk about things, but right now, I'm not in the mood. If you don't mind, I'll be going, and maybe we can talk a little more in the morning.'

Laurel left the man and his sons at their camp near Paradise Creek and rode Angel to the barn on the high ground. In the moonlight, she unsaddled the steeldust and turned him into the paddock. The bundle of blankets and ground cloth, she put in the tack room, along with the saddlebags full of supplies and ammunition. The saddle went on the corral fence and the Winchester leaned against the wall just inside the tack room door. Before spreading the bedding out on the box bunk Jack had built to the wall of the tack room, she took a few minutes to walk to the graves on the hillside. She sat down beside Jack's grave and told him about her day. 'That Robert Dunn is almighty set on buying Paradise,' she said aloud. She paused a long moment, then took a deep breath. 'He'll get our ranch over my dead body, Jack, if he gets it at all.'

'A man and two boys are camping down at the creek. He seemed a good sort, so I said they could stay. He cooks well. I'd better turn in. The sun comes up early and there's a ton of things that need doing here. Goodnight, Jack. I'm lonely without you and the boys. Lonely. Damn lonely. But I'll make out. Somehow. I promise.' The tears in her eyes threatened to keep her from seeing her way back to the barn. Down where the McBrides were camping, the fire was out and the wagon was just a hazy lump against the backdrop of box alders.

Laurel was asleep the moment she lay herself down in those new blankets, and she didn't wake until she heard the rattle of harness just after daybreak. She leaped from the blankets, pulled on her boots, clapped on her floppy hat, and strode to the springhouse to wash her face and hands before getting breakfast ready. The McBride wagon with its brace of big mules stood by the remains of her house when she returned.

'Good morning, Mrs Baker,' Finn said.

Laurel nodded. 'Had breakfast yet?'

'Figured we'd better be on our way,' he said. 'There were some biscuits left over from last night that we'll save for dinner.'

'No breakfast for growing boys? Park the wagon behind the barn where the mules can get some forage. I'll fix you bacon and eggs to go with those biscuits. And boil some coffee.'

'We wouldn't want to impose,' Finn said.

'No imposition. Now park that wagon and send those boys around to help.'

'Yes, ma'am. Will, you and Cal jump off right now and do whatever Mrs Baker asks you to, all right?'

The boys clambered down from the wagon and came to stand before Laurel: one dark-haired and brown eyed; one with light-brown hair, freckles across his nose, an impish grin and twinkling blue eyes.

'Willard. The horses in the paddock are Angel and Molly. Big Red's across the stream. Angel is the steel-dust gelding and Molly is the work mare. You'll find nosebags hanging in the barn, and there are oats in a bin in the granary over there. Put two scoops of oats in each nosebag and give them to the horses. Just let Big Red be. Can you do that?'

Will grinned. 'Yes, ma'am,' he said in perfect imitation of his father. He ran to the barn and soon found the nosebags. Laurel watched him long enough to see that he knew what to do.

'Calvin.'

'Everyone calls me Cal,' the boy said.

'All right. Cal. There are box nests in the chicken coop. Go collect all the eggs from those nests. They should fit in your hat. Don't stumble, though, because you wouldn't want to wear a hat full of gooey eggs, would you?'

Cal giggled at the prospect and raced off to the chicken coop.

Laurel went to the root cellar and cut off a large hunk from the side of bacon hanging there. She'd just gotten back to the fire pit when Finn came back. 'Will's giving the horses their morning bait of oats,' she said, 'and Cal's gathering eggs. They're good boys, Mr McBride.'

'Please call me Finn.'

'All right. My name is Laurel.'

'Very pleased to make your acquaintance, Laurel.'

'Thank you. Would you mind building a small fire, please? It won't take much to fry bacon and eggs,' she said.

Finn walked away to gather wood and Laurel suddenly realized the precarious situation she was in. A woman, alone, with a man she didn't know and two boys who would probably do anything their father ordered them to. Her hands trembled as she set out the frying pan along with the cutting board and a big butcher knife.

Will returned first. 'Horses fed, ma'am,' he said, sounding much older than his eight years.

'Th-thank you, Will. Take a seat on one of those

blocks of wood, please. Your father and Cal should be here soon.'

'Yes, ma'am,' he said. Laurel couldn't help but notice again how the boy was polite and well behaved. Still. . . .

'Will?' she said. 'Does your dad like coffee?'

'Yes'm. But we ain't got none.'

'Do me a special favor, Will?'

The boy nodded.

'You be careful, but in that burned house over there, back by the cook stove somewhere, you'll find a coffee pot. Could you bring it, please?'

This time Will didn't run. He stepped carefully into the ruins of Laurel's home, and made his way to the back of the house.

' 'Leven eggs,' Cal hollered. He came from the chicken coop, walking gingerly and carrying his hat full of eggs as if they might crack of their own accord.

'That should be enough for breakfast,' Laurel said. 'Thank you, Cal.' She took the hatful of eggs from the boy and set them next to the cutting board.

Finn came back with a handful of pine needles and an armload of pine limbs. He put pine needles in the centre and piled shavings around them, topped by small branches. He lit the needles with a lucifer and flames soon licked at the pine branches.

Laurel sliced the bacon into the frying pan and placed it on the fire. 'We like our bacon just short of crisp,' she said. 'I hope that's OK.'

'You're the cook,' Finn said. Cal just grinned.

Will came back from the house with the blackened

coffee pot in hand. He held it out to Laurel.

'Thank you, Will. Just put it down by the fire.' She held out a square of flour sacking to Finn. 'Water for coffee in the spring house, Finn. Could you get three or four cups in the coffee pot?'

'Sure thing.' Finn strode toward the spring house with the blackened coffee pot.

Laurel stepped over to the tack house for her sack of coffee beans and a hammer. By the time Finn returned, she'd crushed a handful of beans on the cutting board. Finn held out the pot and she brushed the crushed beans into it. He set the pot at the edge of the fire.

The bacon was well browned so Laurel put it on a tin plate. She cracked the eggs one after the other and dropped them into the frying pan. Eleven golden yolks jiggled as the bacon grease fried the eggs from the bottom. She sprinkled a little salt over them, and watched as the whites congealed and the yolks gradually cooked. With a knife, she cut the eleven eggs into three portions of three eggs each and one of two. She handed each of the McBrides a tin plate. Holding the frying pan with a hot pot holder she'd made of old flour sacks, Laurel tipped it and slid a three-egg portion onto each tin plate, and the two eggs remaining onto her own. She divided up the bacon and squatted on her heels with her own plate in hand. 'Are you a family that says grace, Mr McBride?' she asked.

'We were, er, not lately, not since—'

'Here we say grace,' Laurel said and bowed her

head. 'Thank you God for food to eat. Bless us to use our strength in doing good. Amen.'

'Amen,' echoed three male voices.

'Please eat,' Laurel said and proceeded to devour the bacon and eggs on her own plate.'

'You're alone,' Finn stated.

After a moment of silence, Laurel said, 'Yes.'

'Can you work this place by yourself?'

'I will.'

Finn looked off down the valley. 'I reckon this valley covers somewheres around six thousand acres.'

'I have title to it all.'

'I've heard tell of white-faced cattle called Herefords that do right well in high country and winter better than most. If you fenced your valley in, I reckon you could do with some white-faced cows.'

'What difference does it make to you, Finn McBride, what I do with my valley?'

Finn looked at her directly. 'Since I lost my Martha and my place in Colorado, me and my boys have wandered mostly, going with the breezes, hauling a wagon load of Mr Glidden's patented barbwire and building fences whenever and wherever people needed them built.'

Finn picked up a stick and drew a rough map of the valley in the dirt by the fire. He took another bite of bacon and stuffed a whole egg in his mouth. After chewing and swallowing, he spoke again. 'I've built a lot of fences, Laurel, and here's how you can make the most of your valley.' He divided the outline of the valley into a series of straight lines, some running parallel to the creek, some perpendicular.

'How does your garden do?' Finn asked.

'Root crops do well, potatoes and carrots and turnips and such. Deer eat the green things like peas and chard and corn. Sometimes they get the tops of the turnips and beets before the roots get a chance to grow. I have to plant about three times as much as I need. The deer and the rabbits know they can get a good feed at the Baker garden,' she smiled ruefully.

'An eight-foot fence around your corn and truck would keep the deer and cattle out. I'll have to think about the rabbits.'

'What's all this talk about fence, Finn McBride?'

Finn ducked his head. 'You say you're going to run this place all alone. I need to build fences so me and my boys can stay alive. Fences can make it so the valley can be handled by one or two people, well, maybe three.'

He straightened up and looked directly at Laurel. 'Big outfits are not fencing much yet. But here, I could make a showpiece about how it's done. Won't you hire me to build the fences you need, Laurel?'

Laurel looked carefully at Finn McBride. He returned her scrutiny with forthright gaze. His clothes were worn, patched, and darned, but his hazel eyes were clear. His face had not felt a razor for some days, and his black hair curled over his ears. The hands that held his tin plate were gnarled and strong. They'd seen more than their share of hard work. They looked like honest hands.

She poured two cups of coffee from the steaming

coffee pot, and handed one tin mug to Finn. 'Consider yourself hired by Paradise's Rafter P brand, Finn McBride. I will pay you cowhand wages, twenty-five a month for you and I'll feed you and your boys, and I'll pay for wire and staples. You'll take care of posts, I reckon. We have no bunkhouse. You can camp by your wagon or bed in the hayloft in the barn. It's up to you.'

The smile on Finn McBride's face made him look almost boyish. 'Thank you, Laurel Baker. You'll not regret this. I swear.' He took a gulp of his coffee, then finished his bacon and eggs with almost unseemly haste.

'Thank you for breakfast, Mrs Baker,' Will said, holding out his empty plate.

'Me, too,' said Calvin with his plate extended as well.

Laurel pointed. 'Will, Cal, there's a dishpan and a crock of soap in that springhouse. And you'll find a dishrag hanging from a nail. Bring them here please.'

The boys scampered off on their errand.

'You'll find buckets in the tack room, Finn. Two buckets of water from the creek, please, after you've finished your coffee.'

'Yes, ma'am.' Finn grinned, drank the remainder of his coffee, and went to fetch the water.

When everything was assembled, Laurel put three inches of water in the pan and set it on the coals of the breakfast fire. She dipped the dishrag in creek water, swiped it over the soap crock, worked it back

and forth in her hands until suds formed, then proceeded to wash all the dishes, including the frying
pan, in a bucket of creek water. 'Here.' Laurel held a
plate out to Will. 'Slosh this in that bucket and put it
in the pan on the fire.'

'I reckon the fire got rid of all my dish towels,'
Laurel said when the dishes were all washed and
rinsed. 'Just pour the water out of the dishpan and
leave the dishes in it.' She pulled the now-dry frying
pan from the coals. 'Will, please bring the dishpan,'
Laurel said, carrying the frying pan to the tack room.
She put the pan and dishes away.

Returning, she said, 'I've got things to do. Finn,
you know fences and how they can be used. Come
with me for a moment so you can see what we've
done with Paradise so far.' She strode to a high point
that overlooked almost the entire valley. Finn followed.

'Paradise Creek starts somewhere up in the White
Mountains,' she said. 'You saw that the water's good.
No alkali. No muck.'

Finn nodded. 'Your valley has all the water it needs
as long as someone doesn't cut it off from above you.'

'I want to grow hay and grain close in. We'll want
to cut grass in the meadows, too, but forty acres of
alfalfa would be about right for hay with another
forty for wheat and oats, I think. I'll want a field for
corn, too. Ten acres of vegetables is more than
enough for me and any ranch hands.'

'Give me some time to ride over the valley and see
what you've got,' Finn said.

'We bought ten sections from Don Alfredo.'

'That's 6,400 acres. Looking at the grass you've got now, I'd say you can run up to 500 cows – well, calves, steers, breeders, and three or four bulls.'

'I can't buy that many cows,' Laura said. 'And I'm in no hurry. A few at a time would be best.'

'I understand,' Finn said.

Laura stared out toward the wagon track. Three horsemen came out of the trees, riding toward the burned-out Paradise ranch house. 'That's Robert Dunn and his men,' she said with a slight tremble in her voice. For a moment she stood as if glued to her tracks. Then she sprinted down the incline toward the tack room and her Yellow Boy Winchester.

CHAPTER SEVEN

'I've been watching your log delivery, Bob,' Fletcher Comstock said. 'Ninety-six on Monday, eighty-seven on Tuesday, and a hundred and three yesterday. Not enough. Not nearly enough.' Comstock leaned back in his chair and stared up at Robert Dunn, who stood in uncomfortable silence in front of Comstock's big desk. He didn't like being called on the carpet. Didn't Comstock know there were always wrinkles to iron out of any operation?

'But Fletch,' he said. 'You don't start sawing for another week or ten days. We can build up a stock for you in that time. Trust me.'

'A hundred and twenty logs a day, Bob, average. You're right. It'll be probably ten more days before we fire up the boiler and start running that buzz saw. That said, I want more than a thousand logs in that pond before we start.'

'You'll have the logs you need, Fletch. I promise.'

Comstock stared at Dunn for a long moment. 'All right, Bob. Let's do it this way. We won't talk pay until a thousand logs float in my log pond. The faster you get the logs in, the faster I'll be inclined to pay for them.'

Dunn took a deep breath. 'All right, Fletch. We had a bargain, and I fully intend to hold up my end of it.'

'You do that, and I'll have no problem,' said Comstock.

Dunn jammed his hat on his head and strode from Comstock's office. Outside, he gathered the reins of his paint gelding, mounted, and rode down Main Street to Mill Road. A wagon piled high with logs rumbled down the East Fork road and turned onto Mill Road ahead of him. He let the paint follow the wagon to the dump-off dock. Dunn watched as the teamster pulled the loaded wagon up about four feet from the edge of the dock, jammed on the brakes, and clambered down from the high seat. Two oak-and-iron side stakes on each side of the wagon held the logs in place, with chains over the top of the load to secure it. The teamster unhooked the chains from the stakes, leaving the middle chain in place to hold the load. He swung the pond-side stakes down to rest on the lip of the dock, then stepped around to the other side of the wagon. He used a lever to undo the centre chain. For a moment, the logs stayed in place. The teamster jiggled the wagon and the logs rolled off the load, down the inclined stakes, and splashed into the pond, leaving only three lying on the wagon bed. He skilfully levered the remaining three until they also rolled off the bed.

'Hey, Brewer,' Dunn called.

'Yeah?'

'How long'd it take you to get here from East Fork?'

'Too long. Had to ride the godamn brake almost all the way. Look at them pads. Just about wore through. Once I get back up on the mountain, they'll have to be replaced.'

'Just tell me how long it took to come down the mountain.'

'Well. The logs was loaded last night and I left camp at daybreak, and I'd better be getting back. Days're getting shorter.'

Dunn pulled a watch from his vest pocket. Almost two o'clock. An eight-hour haul from East Fork. As Brewer turned his wagon around, another load of logs came in, pulled by a six-horse team of Belgians. Less than an hour between loads. He'd forgotten to ask Brewer if he was the number one wagon. 'Hey Sparky,' he called to the second teamster. 'You number two?'

'Hell, no, Mr Dunn. I'm the fourth wagon off the mountain.'

Four wagons unloaded. Six to go. If he was to unload a hundred and twenty logs a day, he'd need more wagons. Damn. A man's money won't last forever. The distance from Ponderosa to Paradise Valley was less than half that to East Fork. If logs could come through Paradise, he wouldn't need more wagons. Dunn turned the paint's head toward Bogtown and Old Glory.

Jinx had Dunn's bottle of Turley's Mill on the bar a few seconds after he'd shouldered open Old Glory's door.

'Afternoon, Mr Dunn. Here's your whiskey.'

Dunn said nothing as he swept the half-full bottle from the bar along with a thick shot glass. He took the rearmost table in the long room and sat with his back to the wall. 'Seen Dirk Rawlins and Red Finney around?' he asked Jinx.

'Ain't been in today, but I reckon they will be. Seem to make it in about every day.'

Dunn poured his first shot of Turley's Mill and threw it back. He grimaced as the 86-proof liquor made its way down his throat to his stomach and into his bloodstream. Felt good. The Baker woman didn't have bandages on her arms or face any more. The scar on her face was unsightly, but all in all, she looked as tough as harness leather. Too bad the boys had gone in the fire. Wasn't intended that way, but things happen. He had a second shot of Turley's Mill.

Dunn took the bottle back to Jinx at the bar. 'I'll come back later,' he said.

'Any time, Mr Dunn,' he said. He stowed the bottle under the counter as Dunn turned away.

Old Glory's looking up, Dunn thought. New lanterns. New mirror behind the bar. New painting on the wall. For a moment he wondered if Alice Murdock had posed for the nude, but shook off the thought. No one in Ponderosa could paint that good.

He pushed the swinging door open. No boardwalk

73

in Bogtown, just a wooden porch that extended across the front of the saloon. He untied his horse's reins and stepped into the saddle. A hundred yards down Corduroy Road, he dismounted and wrapped the reins over the hitching rail in front of Miss Murdock's Institute for Wayward Young Women.

Dunn stepped into the empty parlour. Too early for customers, he thought. He turned full circle, taking in the crystal chandelier, the fine china vase, the overstuffed sofas, the soft beige wallpaper, the carefully burnished spittoons. Obviously, Alice knew how to make things look elegant and expensive. It probably helped increase the prices of her young women's services. Dunn didn't know. As a one-third owner, he never paid.

A young woman in a low-cut dress came from the back room. 'Would you like something to drink, sir?' she asked.

'Tell Alice I'm here,' he said.

'Whom shall I say is calling?'

'Robert Dunn.'

'Thank you, Mr Dunn. I'm sure she will be right out.' The woman went out the same door she'd come in. Dunn sat on the edge of a velvet-covered chair. He crossed his legs one way, and then the other. He stood and stepped over to the hat rack, where he hung his short-brimmed Stetson. He paused a moment before the mirror to brush his curly hair back behind his ears. His reflection showed a slim man of thirty-five with a trim moustache and longish light-brown hair, dressed in grey stripped California pants, ruffled white shirt and black leather vest.

'You look fine, Robert.'

Dunn whirled. He'd not heard Alice enter. 'You shouldn't creep up on a man like that.'

Alice laughed. 'You were too busy inspecting yourself, that's all.'

'Actually, it's more of a business call.'

'How so?'

'I'd like to know how successful our partnership is.'

'Except for a couple of freelance whores working from cribs, we have no competition. Our clientele comes not only from Old Glory, we also get a lower class of person from Charlie's Place and that other bar. Those men know to come to the side door.' Alice paused for a breath.

'We don't let greasy, dirty men through the front door,' she said. 'And the ones that come in the side door can't be with our girls until they've had a bath. That's an extra fifty cents.'

'How many wayward young women are in our institute now?'

'Besides the merchandise you have already inspected?' Alice smiled. 'I'd thought I might be enough for you, but obviously such is not the case.' Her face hardened. 'Five young ladies for gentlemen, an even dozen for the soldiers and sawyers and lumberjacks, and a few in cribs that are hardly worth counting.'

'Sounds like a good foundation for a thriving business.' Dunn rubbed his hands over the seams of his trousers. 'I'll be needing a dividend on my invest-ment soon,' he said.

'Dividends usually come once a year. I put a lot of money into this institute so the payback may not be soon.' Alice's words were as hard as her face.

'If my plans don't work out right, I'll be coming for a dividend. Count on it.' Dunn's voice took on a hard, flat tone, too.

'Come see me when the time comes, Robert. I'll do what I can.' Alice patted her hair. 'Is that all you need today? Or did you want some entertainment as well?'

'I've got to talk to Dirk and Red. I may be back later.'

'Come back for a hot bath. We can talk more leisurely after that.' Alice put her fingers on Dunn's cheek. 'That might work wonders.'

Dunn nodded. 'Could be. We'll see.' He retrieved his hat from the hat rack, placed it carefully on his head, and left by the front door. The paint waited hipshot at the hitching rail. Dunn retrieved the reins and mounted for the short ride back to Old Glory. It sounded like there might not be much money coming from Alice. Maybe he needed a good game of cards. Dunn grew up on the Mississippi, first as a cabin boy on the *Delta Queen* and later as a card dealer on the *Belle of New Orleans*. The card trick he couldn't see had yet to be invented. Few in Ponderosa knew of his past so he rarely played poker. Now he needed money for more wagons. The card tables at Old Glory looked more enticing. A few nights with the pasteboards might turn his luck.

As he intended to stay several hours, Dunn turned the paint into the corral behind Old Glory. He pushed through the swinging door and Jinx had his bottle and a glass on the mahogany by the time Dunn got to the end of the bar.

'Going to make a night of it?' Jinx asked.

'May well do that, Jinx. What're the pasteboards like?'

'Thatcher's the dealer. He's straight. Mr Sims don't want no card sharks at Old Glory. Skill and luck are all that lets you win here.'

Dunn grinned. 'Maybe I'll play a hand or two. Got a new pack of cards?'

Jinx shoved a pack across the bar and Dunn pocketed them. He turned to survey the room. A cowboy and one of the young ladies from Alice's place whispered at the front table. The rear table and the second table were empty. Thatcher sat at the third table playing solitaire. He'd gamble with house money, so anything he lost would come out of Sims's pocket. Dunn poured himself a shot and drank it down. Bottle and glass in hand, he walked over to Thatcher's table. For several minutes he watched the gambler's solitaire. Thatcher played a straight game. No tricks. No shuffling to make sure of a win. Just straight solitaire. Dunn appreciated that.

Without looking up from his cards, Thatcher said, 'Interested in a game?'

'Could be.'

'Have a seat.'

Dunn pulled out a chair across from Thatcher. 'You play a straight game of solitaire,' he said.

'Man that cheats on himself will cheat anyone,' Thatcher replied. 'Like to see if I can beat the cards. Comes out a little better than fifty-fifty.'

Dunn put his new pack of cards on the table. 'Five card stud?'

'I know the game,' Thatcher said.

Dunn broke the pack open. 'Dollar ante,' he said. 'High roller, eh?'

'Been known to be, but I've never played with you and I'd like to break my hand in before things get hot and heavy.'

'Lazy afternoon. Dollar's fine with me. Your deal.'

'Hang on a second.' Dunn stepped to the bar and put down a double eagle. 'Give me some cartwheels, Jinx.'

The 'keep counted out twenty silver dollars. Dunn raked them from the bar and took his seat at the card table. He arranged the cartwheels in four stacks of five. He picked up the deck of cards and shuffled them. Nothing fancy, just a good shuffle, and dealt Thatcher and himself each a hand. Without looking at his cards, he put a dollar in the middle of the table.

Thatcher grinned. He matched the dollar with one of his own. 'Playing the averages, eh?'

'When I deal, I've got as good a chance as you. When you deal, I don't know . . . yet. Right now, I'll go with the averages.'

Dunn won that hand with three nines and his

stacks of cartwheels increased to twenty-five. By the time the sun went down, he'd won some and lost some but was ahead of the game with more than thirty dollars. He gathered the cartwheels in his hands and took them to the bar. 'Three eagles, Jinx,' he said, counting out thirty dollars on the bar. He pocketed the three gold coins and turned back to Thatcher's table. 'Thanks. You play a straight game. One day we'll do it up right.'

'I'll be here,' Thatcher said.

Dunn took his bottle and glass back to the rear table. Old Glory was starting to fill up, and the gabble of voices rumbled at his eardrums. He poured shot and drained it. His bottle of Turley's Mill still had four fingers in the bottom when Dirk and Red pushed their way through the swinging door and bellied up to the bar. Without asking, Jinx poured them each a shot of whiskey, then waved toward Dunn's table. The two men downed their drinks and wandered to the back of the room.

'You looking for us?' Dirk asked.

Dunn nodded. 'Thought you might be in. You ready to take a ride with me in the morning?'

'Worth a drink of that Turley's Mill to you?'

Dunn signalled for two more glasses from Jinx. 'Certainly is,' he said.

'Where we going to ride?' Red asked.

'Paradise,' Dunn said.

CHAPTER EIGHT

Laurel stood between the tack room and the ruins of her house, waiting for Robert Dunn and his riders to approach. She held the Winchester casually in the crook of her arm, but it was cocked and ready to fire. The red scar on her face stretched from hairline to the curve of her jaw, and her eyes were slits as she watched Dunn and his men. They rode with their hands on their saddlehorns, away from their firearms.

'Good morning, Missus Baker,' Dunn said, putting a finger to the brim of his hat.

Laurel said nothing, her face hard and her stance ready for trouble. Her lip lifted in a snarl that said if this man wanted her land, she would defend it to death.

Finn McBride stepped out from the barn door, a shovel in his hand and no gun in sight. 'Howdy,' he said. 'Breakfast is over. I reckon you'll have to go without.'

'Who the hell are you?' Dunn said, his voice flat and toneless.

'What's it to you?'

Dunn growled. 'Don't like your attitude, stranger. Shut up and stand out of the way.'

'Missus Baker invited us to camp for the night. We'll move when she says to, and not before,' Finn said.

'Us?'

'Me and my boys.'

Dunn scanned quickly left and right. 'Where are they?'

'I tell them to stay out of sight when strangers come around. You could look, but I don't reckon you'd find them.'

'I don't reckon that makes any difference.' Dunn turned his attention back to Laurel, but McBride walked over to stand in front of Dunn's paint horse. He leaned on the shovel.

'Mister, I'm thinking Missus Baker is not happy you're here. Could I suggest that you turn your horses around and leave?' McBride stood up straight and hefted the shovel in his hand.

'Boss?' Red Finney's hand shifted from the saddle-horn toward his gun.

'Easy, Red. I just want to talk to Missus Baker. No need for gunplay.'

Laurel stood stock still, her back straight and her legs spraddled. In jeans, with her knife-scarred face and her body squared off by a wide-shouldered mackinaw, she looked mean and tough, like old rawhide.

She growled. 'What do you want, Dunn?'

'A word. A proposal, if you will.'

'I don't reckon that means you want to marry me, does it.'

'No, ma'am. As I mentioned before, I'd like to buy your ranch. Without your family, you really have no need for this property. You'd be much better off in town – Ponderosa or Tombstone or even San Francisco.'

'I won't leave the Rafter P,' Laurel said through clenched teeth.

'Hear me out. I'll offer four dollars an acre. That's more than twenty-five thousand dollars,' said Dunn. His expression bled honeyed honesty. 'Use the money well, and you'll never have to work again.'

'I like work. I like building a life on my land. I've lived in Paradise, I'll die in Paradise ... when the time comes.'

'Think about it, Missus Baker. Think about it carefully. I'll come back when you've had some time to consider.' Dunn reined his paint around. 'There are ways I could have this land for nothing, you know,' he said over his shoulder. 'Think on it.' He clucked to the paint, which started down the wagon track toward Ponderosa at a leisurely walk. The two riders followed.

'I don't like that man,' Finn said.

'Nor do I. He wants Paradise godawful bad.' Laurel let the hammer of the Winchester down. 'You got a short gun?'

'Yes.'

'You'd better carry it. A bullet carries a bit farther than the blade of a shovel.' Laurel smiled. 'Thanks for coming out, but I could have handled Dunn alone.'

'Maybe. This time.'

'I turned him around before,' she said, 'I can do it again.' She strode toward the tack room. 'I've got potatoes to plough up.' Leaning the Winchester against the wall, she took a harness from its pegs and threw it over her shoulder. She retrieved the Winchester and went to harness Molly. Hanging the harness over the paddock fence and leaning the Winchester against it, Laurel took a bridle into the paddock and walked straight at Molly. The big horse took a few steps around in a circle, then seemed to decide there was no way to escape. She turned her left side to Laurel and waited.

Laurel stepped quietly up to the work mare, running a hand over her back and up her withers. She looped a length of rein leather around Molly's neck, then settled the bridle in place, giving Molly time to accept the bit and get used to the idea that today was a work day. Then she led the gentle mare over to the paddock fence and harnessed her for the day's work.

Finn stood at the gate. 'What shall I do?'

'What must you do to build fences?'

'I'd like to walk all your land.'

Laurel pointed up Paradise Creek toward the place where it left the trees and started its winding way through the valley. 'The land runs a mile north and south on either side of Paradise Creek from where the stream comes out in the open. The south line runs to Paradise Gorge, then the west line goes two miles north until it connects with the north boundary. You'd better take a horse.'

'I'll walk it, if you don't mind. Gives me a better feel of the land.'

Laurel looked uncomfortable. 'Finn, I'm not good at taking care of children. You can see what happened to mine.'

'Hey, Pa.' Will's call came from the barn loft. 'Can we come out now?'

'All right, boys,' Finn said. 'You can help Missus Baker.' The youngsters came scrambling from the barn. Finn looked directly at Laurel's eyes. She met his eyes for a long moment, then dropped her gaze as a bit of colour crept into her cheeks. 'What happened to your boys was an accident,' Finn said. 'Don't let it smother you. I trust you with my sons.'

Laurel swallowed at the lump in her throat. It didn't go away. She swiped a sleeve at the tears that threatened to overflow her eyes. She gulped. The two McBride boys stood by their father, waiting for her to say something.

'Will. . . .' Laurel cleared her throat and started again. 'Will. In the granary, you will find some gunny sacks folded and hung on one of the partitions. Bring me four, please.'

'Yes'm.' The boy sprinted away on his errand.

Laurel and Finn stood in uncomfortable silence. Then Cal said, 'Do I get to do something?'

Finn laughed. 'A big feller like you? Missus Baker's likely to have you lugging heavy loads. I heard her say she's gonna plough for spuds.'

'Plough for spuds?'

'That's right. She'll use the moldboard and old Molly to turn up the spuds. You and Will can get the potatoes out and fill up them sacks. That right, Missus Baker?'

Laurel's smile trembled a bit. 'That's exactly right, Mr McBride, exactly.'

'Wow.' Cal's eyes sparkled at the prospect of doing a useful job.

'I got the gunny sacks!' Will shouted, bursting from the granary door. He skidded to a halt in front of Laurel. 'Here,' he said, holding out the sacks.

Laurel cut two with her clasp knife so she could tie the strips left at the edges and let the rest hang down, like a horse's nosebag. She hung one over Will's shoulders and the other on Cal. She shortened the strips on Cal's so it wouldn't drag the ground. 'I'll ride Molly across the creek,' she said. 'You boys go across the footbridge upstream.'

Across the creek, Laurel hitched Molly to the moldboard plough and let her drag it to the potato patch. She set the plough at the edge of the plot. With her hands on the handles and the reins around her shoulders, she spoke to the mare. 'Let's go, Molly,' she said. The mare put her shoulders to the harness collar and the ploughshare bit into the loamy soil. Laurel ploughed a straight furrow down the length of the field, turned, and ploughed another down the far side. Will and Cal stood at the edge of the potato patch, not sure what to do.

'Whoa, Molly,' Laurel said. 'Hey, Will, Cal, see all those potatoes I turned up?'

The boys nodded.

'Some will still be buried, but when you pick up the ones you can see, the roots will lead you to the ones you can't. Get them all and put them in those sacks over your shoulders, OK?'

'Yes'm,' the boys chorused.

'When your bags get heavy, bring them back here and dump your loads into the other gunny sacks. We put those in the root cellar and they'll last till spring. OK. You know what to do, get to it.' As she looked toward the trees, she saw Finn McBride disappearing into them. This time, he had a gunbelt strapped around his hips. Laurel gulped. She and the two boys were across the creek without any protection. What if Dunn and his gunnies came back? Laurel tipped the plough on its side and took off the reins. 'Stay, Molly,' she said, and raced for the tack room, splashing and high-stepping across the creek because she didn't want to spend the extra time going upstream to the footbridge.

As she sprinted for the tack room, she felt panic welling. Finn McBride trusted her with his two sons but she wasn't even able to protect her own. The sad burnt faces of Jimmy and Jason crowded into her brain, bringing tears to her eyes. She shook her head. No time to pine over losses. No time. Her breath came in gasps. The door wouldn't open, no matter how hard she pushed. Why? Why? Then she remembered the door swung outward. She jerked it open. The Yellow Boy Winchester stood against the wall where she'd left it. Ready, with a full magazine and a cartridge in the chamber. All she had to do was thumb back the hammer and pull the trigger. She reached for the rifle. It felt warm in her hands, almost alive. A tiny smile crept across her lips. She stood taller and felt safer. She tucked the rifle under her arm and left the tack room.

Outside, she stopped for a moment to check her surroundings. No horses showed on the wagon track. Finn McBride was nowhere to be seen. Will and Cal searched the ploughed furrows for potatoes, their bags slowly filling. Molly stood in her traces, the picture of patience. Laurel's heartbeat slowed to normal. She went to the saddle on the paddock fence and removed the Winchester's scabbard. Shoving the rifle into it, she laid it across her shoulder and waded back across the creek. She tied the scabbard across the handles of the plough, then snaked the Winchester out and brought it to her shoulder. The move went smoothly. She could be armed in a moment if she needed to be.

'Giddyup, Molly. You've had more than enough rest.' The McBride boys had started down the second row, so Laurel aligned Molly just uphill of the first row and ploughed another furrow that turned into the first one. The potatoes looked round and firm. They'd be good come winter.

Laurel and the boys worked until the sun was high.

'Come on,' she called to the boys as she slipped the traces. 'Time for dinner.' She led Molly across the creek, took off her bridle, and gave her a nosebag with a quart of oats in it. Laurel then made a quick dinner of frybread and bacon for herself and the boys. 'Haven't milked the cows lately,' she said. 'So you'll have to do with water from the springhouse.'

'I'll get it,' Will said, and scampered off.

Laurel watched him go and the ache for Jimmy and Jason returned. She ached while they ate, and she ached as they worked through the afternoon. Her heart still hurt as she sliced new potatoes and well-cured bacon into the frying pan for supper. The sun went down and still no sign of Finn McBride.

With supper finished, some set aside for Finn, and the dishes washed, Laurel and the boys sat staring at the fire.

'When's Pa coming back?' asked Cal. 'He don't usually leave us alone at dark.'

'What smells so good?' Finn's voice came from out of the dark. 'You all should know better than to stare into the fire. Do that and your night vision is shot.'

'Fried potatoes with bacon,' Laurel said. 'The boys filled four sacks with potatoes today. Maybe you could help get them into the root cellar in the morning.' She paused. 'You're right about staring at the fire,' she said. 'We'll not do it again.'

Finn smiled. 'Good,' he said. 'People like us always need to see the best we can. Not saying it will always be that way, but right now, let's be extra careful. Those new potatoes were delicious, by the way.'

'They'll taste even better come March or April,' Laurel said.

Finn banked the fire. 'Let's go to bed, boys. Up into the loft with you.'

Neither Will nor Cal complained. Harvesting potatoes all day made them more than ready for bed. They sprinted for the barn. Finn stood up. ' 'Night, Laurel. From what I could see today, Paradise is the right name for your place.'

' 'Night, Finn,' she said. In the tack room, she laid the Winchester on the floor by the box bunk, one cartridge in the chamber, fifteen in the magazine. Sleep came quickly and deeply until the clatter and clank of pans startled her awake. She grabbed the Winchester and eased the tack room door open. It squeaked faintly and Laurel told herself she must remember to grease the hinges. The banked fire gave off a little smoke just visible in the moonlight. Across the fire, where Laurel had stacked the frying pans, Dutch ovens, and tin plates and cups in a wooden box, a large black shape snuffled at the utensils, pushing them back and forth with its snout. Laurel fired three shots with the Winchester, aiming above the huge bear. It stood up on its hind legs, sniffing the air.

'Get out of here, Slewfoot,' Laurel yelled.

Finn came from the barn door, pulling up his trousers as he ran. 'Where are they?' he hollered.

'It's just a bear,' Laurel said. The big animal lowered itself to all fours as Finn ran up to Laurel. It rumbled discontent in its great chest, then turned and lumbered back into the pines, favouring its left hind leg.

'I hadn't thought of Slewfoot,' Laurel said. 'He's trying to put on weight before the snow flies. He comes looking for food sometimes. He'll usually go away if you shoot a couple of times and holler at him.'

Finn took a big breath. 'Will he be back tonight?'

'Not likely. He limps on that hind leg, but I still wouldn't want to meet up with him on a dark trail.' Laurel walked over to the scattered utensils. 'Better put these in a stall rather than leaving them out by the fire.' She picked up a Dutch oven by its wire bail and carried it into the barn.

Once the utensils were in the far stall, Laurel stood for a moment outside the tack room, listening. The night was still. 'Can't hear Slewfoot,' she said.

'Gone, I reckon, but we'd best be careful,' Finn said.

'Yes. Goodnight again.'

'Sleep well. I'll be walking again tomorrow. Hope you don't mind keeping the boys here again.'

'They're good boys, and lots of help. We'll get work done, the three of us. See you in the morning.'

Laurel and Finn stood side by side for a moment, looking at the Ponderosa pines on the hill. Laurel stepped to the tack room door. She took a deep breath. 'Get your rest, Finn,' she said, and closed the door.

CHAPTER NINE

Late September gets crisp in the high mountain country. Hoar frost whitened the meadows when Laurel rose in the predawn hours to prepare a breakfast of biscuits, bacon, and eggs for Finn and the boys. She'd separated the milk cows from their calves and Will McBride took pride in milking the two gentle Jersey cows, morning and night. Robert Dunn had not appeared again at Paradise, but Finn found footprints of horses and places where men lay out under the pines at points overlooking the Rafter P.

'Finn,' Laurel said as she finished chewing a mouthful of biscuit and bacon, 'it's good that we've got the root crops in, but we need to put in a store of wood for winter. And we need to cut and stack hay in the meadow so the horses and cows will have feed when the snow flies.'

Finn nodded, his mouth full.

'I can cut hay,' she said. 'You and the boys get wood, OK?'

Laurel was still straining and separating the

morning milking when Finn left with his mules and his sons. She put the drinking milk to cool in the springhouse. The rest she left for the cream to rise. There would soon be enough for a batch of butter.

She spent the day across the creek cutting tall grass. She didn't stop swinging the sharp scythe until the sun disappeared behind the tall Ponderosa pines west of her home. The cut grass would cure in the autumn sun, and they could all work at forking it into a high stack of winter feed.

'Sure would be good to have some trout for supper,' Laurel said, and Will and Cal ran to get their willow fishing poles from the barn. Native trout thrived in Paradise Creek, so the boys returned with half a dozen ten-inchers before the cooking fire was down to coals.

'You've got a clasp knife, son,' Finn said to Will. 'Go clean the fish.'

'I know, Pa,' Will said. 'Just give me a little time, OK. Come on, Cal.' The boys trotted upstream to a shallow spot above the footbridge.

Finn stiffened. 'Don't look now,' he said from the corner of his mouth, 'but Apaches are standing at the treeline.'

He started to draw his revolver, but Laurel put a hand on his arm. 'They're friends,' she said. 'Let them come to the fire.'

The Apaches stepped out of the darkness. Four men and a woman. One of the men carried a haunch of venison over his shoulder. He held the meat out to Finn but spoke to Laurel. 'It is good for you to have a man,' he said. 'We have seen him walking your land. He looks careful, sees much. But he has not seen those who watch you at night.'

Finn stood motionless, holding the haunch of venison. Laurel's hands leaped up to cover her mouth. 'Who? Who watches at night?' she said, her voice trembling.

'White men. Sometimes one. Sometimes two. Creep. Lie beneath the pines. Watch.'

'P'tone, how long have you been watching Paradise?' Laurel asked.

The tall Apache answered. 'We watch since your house burned because we didn't watch.'

'You don't have to do that. I'm strong. Finn and his sons are here. But thank you so much.'

'You and your man who is gone were friends to Alchesay. His people are cousins to my people. His friends are friends of mine. We watch.'

'Will you eat with us?'

P'tone smiled. 'You cook. We eat.'

'Wonderful.' She turned to Finn. 'You slice steaks from that venison. I'll peel potatoes and onions. We'll have a feast. We can fry the boys' fish in the morning.'

The Apaches sat cross-legged on the ground, waiting. Laurel commanded Finn and the boys like drudges, preparing a decent meal for the relatives of her Chiricahua friends.

The meal was cordial, but both Apaches and whites spent little time in conversation as they wolfed venison seasoned with salt and sage, potatoes and onions with bits of chilli peppers to add piquancy to the smooth taste of Jersey butter, biscuits spread with honey, and plenty of strong black coffee for the adults. The boys drank milk.

After the meal, Will finally found his voice. 'Are you a real Apache chief?' he asked.

P'tone smiled. 'Some call me chief. Some of our people even listen to me.'

'Could I see your house?' Cal asked.

'Ask your father,' P'tone said.

Cal turned to Finn. 'Can I, Pa?'

Finn looked uncomfortable. He looked at P'tone, then at Laurel. Neither gave him a hint of expression. He took a deep breath. 'Yes, you may visit Chief P'tone's village, but after all the harvesting is done. OK?'

Cal looked a little scared. 'Could Will come, too?'

'Ask Chief P'tone,' Finn said, a hint of a smile on his lips.

'Chief, can my brother come, too?' Cal asked the staid Apache.

P'tone nodded. 'You both come. Later.' He looked at Laurel. 'Good food,' he said. 'We leave now, but we watch. You watch too. I think those white men no good.'

Laurel shook hands with each of the Apaches and stood watching as they disappeared into the pines.

'You've got interesting friends,' Finn said.

'Good friends,' she said. 'Their medicine women delivered my two sons. All we ever did was treat them like ordinary folks. Fierce fighters they are. Savages they are not.'

'I thought those tracks meant people were looking us over,' Finn said. 'With what the Apaches say, maybe we'd better post watches at night.'

Laurel cleared away the dishes and put them in a tub so the boys could wash them. 'The dishes are ready to do, boys. Then off to bed with you.' She lowered her voice. 'I'll keep watch until midnight. You watch until five, that's when I get up anyway. All right?'

'OK,' Finn said, his face serious in the dying light of the fire.

The supper utensils washed and dried, the McBride boys carried the tub full of pots and pans and plates and cups and tableware into the barn. 'G'night Pa, g'night Laurel,' they called, and climbed to their hayloft bedroom.

Finn stood near the coals of the fire for a long moment. 'Take care, Laurel,' he said. 'Find a place that gives you a good view but keeps you out of sight. Don't move until you call me for my turn.'

'Finn McBride, you sound like you think I've never stood a watch at night, but I have . . . more than once. I can do the job.'

'Just don't want you to get hurt,' Finn mumbled. 'Call me at midnight.' He slouched away to the barn like a boy who'd been scolded.

In the last of the firelight, Laurel wiped her Winchester with a cloth. She checked the magazine to make sure it was fully loaded, then jacked a cartridge into the chamber and added another one to the magazine. Sixteen shots. She'd never fired more than three at a time, but she felt better with the gun fully loaded. She let the hammer down to the half-cock safety position.

In the tack room, she found the toolbox by feel. Her fingers touched the cold steel of the old Dragoon revolver that Jack had converted to .45-calibre shells. The same toolbox yielded a box of .45 rounds. She slipped one into each hole in the cylinder, and put a handful into the pocket of her mackinaw.

Laurel chose a big Ponderosa with a spread of Manzanita at its foot as her lookout nest. She hauled two saddle blankets from the tack room, one to sit on and one to put over her shoulders. The thick Navajo-woven blankets were the warmest things in Paradise, save a blazing pine fire.

Slewfoot came as Laurel watched, snuffing around the banked fire for scraps. After a few minutes, he left, grumbling to himself because he'd found nothing to eat. Laurel could hear him moving through the pines for several minutes, then all went quiet again, except for the click of beetles and the little scratching sounds squirrels made as they searched for pine nuts.

From her nest under the Ponderosa, Laurel could see most of Paradise Valley. The details were indistinct, but the moonlight shone silver on the meadow grass and the creek sparkled with reflected light. The Jerseys were in the barn with hay in their mangers. The black outline of the barn hid the calves from sight. Molly and Angel grazed side by side, and Finn's mules stood at the far end of the paddock. A dark splotch showed in the meadow across the creek – Big Red, Jack's sorrel stallion. Laurel had let him run free, knowing he'd not go far from home. She'd have to bring him in when the snows came; maybe before.

Laurel drew the thick wool saddle blanket over her shoulders and head to ward off the cold, leaving only her nose exposed. Paradise was at peace.

Leaden weights tugged at Laurel's eyelids. She fought to stay alert, to guard her land, but still she slipped toward sleep. Watch! Watch! Stay on guard! She pinched the back of her left hand, digging her thumbnail into the flesh. The pain kept her awake for a few moments.

Her eyes flew open as Slewfoot roared from some-where back in the pines. A shot sounded. Another. The bear roared again and crashed through under-brush. A scream vibrated in the forest. Slewfoot growled, and another scream pierced the night, this time ending in a gurgle. Any semblance of sleep fled Laurel's brain, but she stayed in her lookout nest. She heard the bear moving away, making much more noise than usual. Still she stayed put.

'Get your man,' a low voice said. 'I stay here.' One of P'tone's men stood in the shadows of the big pine.

'What happened?' Laurel whispered.

'Get the man.'

Laurel walked to the barn, Winchester in hand and Dragoon Colt weighing down the pocket of her mackinaw. Once inside the door she called out.

'Finn. Finn.' She kept her voice low.

'Laurel? Is it midnight?' Finn's voice sounded alert.

'Something's happened. Please come.'

In moments, Finn was at Laurel's side. 'Lead on,' he said.

'Pa?' Will's sleepy voice came from the loft.

'Everything's OK, boys. Just stay put,' Finn said.

' 'K.'

Laurel took Finn by the sleeve and led him to her nest by the big Ponderosa. The Apache stood in the shadow, nearly invisible.

'What's this?' Finn asked.

'He wants to show us something,' Laurel said.

The Indian walked away, assuming the others would follow. Laurel hurried after him. Finn sighed, then went along. The Apache turned parallel to the tree line, going southeast up the mountain. He moved as if walking on feathers, in total silence. Laurel winced as her boot came down on a dry twig that cracked like a pistol shot. Finn did little better. Laurel could hear him lumbering along behind.

'There,' the Apache said, pointing at a large lump on the ground.

Laurel crept nearer. The old black bear had mauled the man badly before fastening its jaws at the joint of neck and shoulder. The man's head lay at an odd angle. No blood flowed now. His hat hung precariously from a nearby clump of Manzanita. His right hand still clutched an Army Colt. He was dead.

'The bear bleeds,' said the Apache. 'We will watch

98

him. If he lives, he may become a man killer. If we must, we will kill him.'

'It's Red Finney,' Laurel said. 'One of the riders who always come with Robert Dunn.'

'Looks like he met up with something he couldn't handle,' Finn said. 'What say we take him into Ponderosa and see if we can shake some trees. Help me carry the dead man,' he said to the Indian.

The two men carried the limp body of Red Finney from the forest and laid it out on the bed of Finn's wagon. 'Thank you,' Laurel said. 'I don't even know your name.'

'My people call me Gondalay,' he said.

'Gondalay.' The name had a ring to it. 'Thank you for watching, my friend,' she said.

'We watch. You sleep,' Gondalay said. He glided back into the forest.

Finn got a piece of canvas from the barn and covered Finney's body with it. 'I've got a feeling Mr Dunn's not going to be pleased at losing one of his scouts. Laurel, this may be the start of something serious. We'll need to be loaded and primed for whatever comes.'

'I know, Finn. I'm glad you're here, though I'd fight by myself if it came to that.' Laurel laid her hand on Finn's arm. 'We'll need to make sure the boys don't get in harm's way. They're strong boys, but this is grown-up trouble.'

'We'll see when we get to Ponderosa,' Finn said. 'G'night again.'

' 'Night.'

Laurel got up in the cold of the false dawn to fix their regular breakfast of biscuits and bacon. She got the six fish from the springhouse, sprinkled them with salt, dredged them in flour, and set them to frying in the leftover bacon grease. 'Come and get it or I'll throw it out,' she hollered.

Moments later the boys came racing from the barn. Finn McBride followed at a more leisurely pace. 'Wow. Really smells good,' Will crowed. He grabbed a tin plate and a fork from the chuck box and rushed to the fire.

'Just hang on there,' Laurel said. 'You know we say grace before we eat.'

Will screeched to a stop. Cal whipped off his hat. Finn removed his, too, as did Will.

'Dear God,' Laurel said. 'We thank thee for food to eat. Bless it to give us strength. Amen.'

'Amen,' Finn and the boys chorused, and Will dived for the Dutch oven. He forked a golden-brown trout from the cast-iron utensil and placed it on his plate. He added a biscuit and two slices of bacon. Laurel poured him a cup of milk to go with his breakfast. Will worried a piece of flesh from the trout and stuffed it into his mouth. 'Umm hmm. That's got to be the best trout I ever tasted. We always just stick willows through them and roast them over the fire.'

Laurel smiled. 'Glad you like it,' she said.

With breakfast finished and the dishes washed and put away, Finn hitched the mules to his wagon.

'We're going to Ponderosa today,' he said. 'There's a dead man in the wagon, so you boys stand up by the seat.' The boys sidled around the body, eyes wide and mouths clamped shut. They stood quietly behind the high seat, almost bursting with questions. Finn waved at the body. 'Killed by a bear,' he said. 'We're taking him in to Ponderosa.' He signalled Laurel to climb aboard. She did, with the fully loaded Winchester under her arm and the old Dragoon pistol sagging her mackinaw pocket.

Laurel sat on the high seat while Finn drove the mule team. Neither said anything until the wagon was on the downhill stretch leading into Ponderosa. 'What are we going to do with the body?' Laurel said.

'It's Dunn's man. I say we turn the body over to him.'

'I suppose that's the thing to do. I don't really look forward to confronting him, though.'

'In the middle of Ponderosa? We'll be all right.'

Finn drove the wagon down Corduroy Road, then onto Main. They skirted the bluff overlooking Comstock Sawmill, and passed Gardner's Mercantile. The Comstock Hotel and Jimmy's Kitchen stood on the uphill side of the street. A new building just west of the hotel had EXAMINER painted on its window. Main followed the bluff edge around until it turned into Oak Street where it crossed Corduroy Road again. Another new building stood at the corner of Main and Corduroy. A stocky man in a frock coat and striped britches with black hair curling from under his plainsman's hat stood on the porch. His coat bulged over a revolver on his hip, and he carried a double-barreled shotgun in the crook of his arm.

'Howdy, folks,' he said as the wagon came abreast. 'Good to see you in Ponderosa. I'm Braxton Webber, the new town marshal.'

'Pull up, Finn,' Laurel said. 'Good morning, Marshal,' she said as the wagon came to a halt. 'It's about time we got some law in Ponderosa. I'm Laurel Baker, owner of the Rafter P on Paradise Creek. We have a dead man in our wagon.'

CHAPTER TEN

Marshal Webber snapped the ten-gauge closed and stepped down into the street in front of the mules. He stalked around the animals to face the teamster. Laurel watched him with careful eyes. Her own rifle lay across her lap.

'Don't believe I heard your name,' Webber said to Finn.

'Finn McBride, Marshal. And these are my sons, Will and Cal.'

'What are you doing in Ponderosa?'

'Delivering a dead man.' Finn replied calmly to the marshal's sharp questions.

Laurel spoke. 'We could have left him to rot in the forest, Marshal. But he's a man I've seen riding with Robert Dunn, and I wanted Dunn to know Red Finney is dead.'

Webber raised an eyebrow. 'Well then, maybe I'd better take a look at your dead man.'

'He's not mine,' Laurel retorted, 'nor did I or any of mine have a thing to do with his death.'

'Just the same, I'd like to take a look at the body.'

'I'll help,' Finn said. He handed Laurel the reins and climbed down from the wagon. 'Be best if I let the tailgate down,' he said, his tone of voice still calm and even.

Webber nodded.

Finn took the pins from the tailgate hasps and opened the gate, letting it hang nearly to the ground. He reached in and pulled the canvas tarp off Red Finney's body.

Webber climbed up into the wagon bed for a closer look. 'Looks like he tangled with the wrong end of a catamount,' the marshal said.

'Bear,' said Finn.

Webber pointed at the Colt held in Finney's death grip. 'How's the bear?'

'Wounded.'

'Bad?'

'Dunno. Missus Baker heard two shots. Blood showed with the bear sign. Wound didn't slow the old boy down any that we could see.'

The marshal lifted his hat and scratched at his head. 'Sounds like you've seen the bear before.'

'People around Paradise call him Slewfoot. Big black bear with a hind leg that doesn't sit right. Maybe broke once and healed off-kilter,' Finn said. 'He'll come around looking for scraps and so on, but usually high tails it if you shoot off a couple of rounds and holler a bit.'

'How come you to find Finney?'

'I heard a couple of shots,' Laurel said. 'Slewfoot roared loud and angry like. Then someone screamed.

104

By the time we got there, the old bear was gone and Finney lay dead with his Colt in hand.'

'Bear got away, then?'

'He was gone,' Finn said. 'Morning showed signs of blood, so at least one of Finney's shots hit Slewfoot. Don't know if he crawled off to die or just got a flesh wound. Either way, he's gone into the mountains.' Finn eyed the marshal. 'What do you want us to do with the body?'

Webber scratched his head again. He looked at Laurel and said, 'Would you mind taking it back down Main to Doc Huntly's place? We'll have the doc verify the cause of death, though it looks plain to see, and I'll see if I can dig up Mr Dunn.'

Laurel nodded. 'We can do that,' she said. 'I'd like to be sure Dunn knows where and how his gun hand died.'

Marshal Webber sent a sharp look toward Laurel when she said 'gun hand', but made no comment. 'Dan,' he called.

A gangly teenager came from the office. 'Yes sir, Marshal,' he said.

'This here's Dan Brady. He's too young to deputize so I let him run errands,' Webber said. 'Dan, you look for Bob Dunn. Try Jimmy's Kitchen, Comstock Lumber, and if he's not there, go down to Old Glory. This time of the day, I don't reckon he's still in bed. Anyway, if you don't find him, go ask Bucktooth Alice if she knows.'

'Right away, Marshal.' The boy turned to run down Main.

'Oh, Dan,' Webber called. 'when you find him, tell him I'd like to see him at Doc Huntly's.'

Brady waved a hand and trotted down the street toward the Comstock Hotel and Jimmy's Kitchen.

Finn covered the body with the tarp, raised the tailgate, and slipped the pins into the hasps. He climbed back up on the high seat. 'You did well, boys,' he said. 'Proud of you.' He drove the team forward to the crossroad and turned the rig around. Moments later, he drew the team to a stop in front of a small building with a shingle that read, Vernon Huntly MD.

Laurel climbed off the rig and went into Doc Huntly's place. A cowbell donged as she opened the door. A slight man with greying hair and a neatly trimmed moustache came from a back room.

'Hello, Missus Baker. What may I do for you?' he asked, peering at Laurel over his wire-rimmed spectacles.

'Got a dead man out in the wagon,' Laurel said. 'Marshal Webber wants you to take a look and maybe say what killed him.'

'Dead man, eh? Well, let's see.' He picked up his black bag and held the door open for Laurel to go ahead.

Finn had the tailgate down and the tarp off Red Finney's body. He'd placed a box where Doc Huntly could step on it to get up into the wagon bed. The two boys still stood with their backs against the high seat in front. They watched the doctor's every move.

Doc Huntly tried to flex one of Finney's arms. It

106

wouldn't bend. 'Hmmm. Maximum rigor mortis,' he said. 'Died twelve to fourteen hours ago, then.'

He got a pair of scissors from the bag and proceeded to cut away Finney's shirt. The body had two major claw tracks on its abdomen. One started just above the hip and nearly disembowelled Finney. The other ripped across his chest from shoulder to lower rib cage. Old Slewfoot's claw rips laid the flesh open to the bone.

'My, my,' Doc Huntly said. 'He'd have soon been dead from the claw rips without medical attention.'

The doctor turned his attention to the bite at the juncture of neck and shoulder. 'Bit and shook,' he said. 'Broke his neck. Most people die from loss of blood in animal attacks. This man died of a broken neck.' The doctor straightened, wiped his scissors and put them away. 'Don't know what else I can say.' He shook his head. 'Hell of a way to die.'

Webber arrived. 'Well?' he said to Doc Huntly.

'As I said, dead of a broken neck caused by the bite of a large animal, probably a bear. I'd say he died no more than fifteen hours ago, no less than twelve.'

'Marshal. Marshal.' The kid Dan Brady ran toward the wagon from the direction of Comstock Lumber. He skidded to a halt by Finn's wagon. 'Mr Dunn said he'd be right here.'

Robert Dunn's dapper form appeared at the corner of Walnut Ave and Main. He strode purposefully toward the small crowd now gathered at the McBride wagon. Laurel flipped her Winchester over so its muzzle pointed in Dunn's general direction, but Dunn's eyes were on Braxton Webber.

'What's going on, Marshal?' he said as he approached.

'One of your men got himself killed on my property,' Laurel said, her voice hard and brittle. 'What was he doing there in the middle of the night?'

Dunn ignored Laurel. 'Who is it?' he asked Webber.

'Missus Baker says his name is Red Finney,' Webber said.

Dunn turned to face Laurel. 'Who shot Red?' he said, his words pitched low and menacing. Finn took a step toward Dunn.

'No one,' Laurel replied. 'He got killed by a bear. But that doesn't answer why he was sneaking around the Rafter P in the middle of the night. What was he doing?'

Dunn's face turned into a picture of innocence. 'How could I know what he was doing? He only works for me job by job. It's not like he was on salary.'

Webber considered Dunn for a long moment. 'Seems everyone in town thinks he's your man. So I reckon I'll just turn the body over to you and let you deal with it.'

Dunn sputtered.

'Where do you want this dead man delivered, Dunn. I'll do that much,' Finn said.

'I'd prefer that Mr Dunn pick up Finney right here,' Laurel said. 'We hauled him all the way from Paradise. No need to go any farther. I'll give you an hour to get things organized, Mr Dunn. If you've not removed the body from our wagon by then, we'll dump it on the street and go back to Paradise.'

'OK, OK.' Dunn threw up both hands. 'Someone will come to get Red as soon as I can arrange it.'

'Dunn!' Finn's voice knifed the air. 'Why was that man sneaking through the underbrush south-west of Missus Baker's place on Paradise?'

Dunn shrugged. 'I have no way of knowing.'

'I think you do.'

'Think all you want, McBride. I don't know.'

Finn walked up to Dunn, crowding him closely. 'If I find out you lied, Dunn, I'll kill you personally,' he said.

'McBride. Don't go around threatening Ponderosa's citizens,' the marshal said. 'Let him go. He's got to get rid of this body. It'll soon start to ripen.' Webber waved a hand. 'Get on about it, Dunn. Your hour's ticking away.'

Dunn rushed off.

'Hold on to your temper, McBride,' Webber said. 'If he's in the wrong, he'll show his hand soon enough.'

Finn shoved his hands into his mackinaw pockets. 'Yeah, I guess you're right. It's just that he's got no call to push Laurel so hard.'

'Push?'

'Yeah. Dunn wants her land.'

'That right, Missus Baker?' Marshal Webber asked.

'He brought gunmen when he offered to buy me out,' she said. 'Seemed to be in an awful hurry to clinch the deal.'

109

Laurel took a coin from her pocket. 'Here, Will,' she said. 'Take this nickel and go over to Gardner's with your brother and see if you can't find something good. Don't be too long, though. We'll be leaving soon.'

'Gee. Thanks, Laurel. Come on, Cal!' The boys scrambled from the wagon and ran up the boardwalk toward Gardner's Mercantile. Laurel's eyes followed the boys, then brimmed with tears that she wiped away with the sleeve of her mackinaw.

'You didn't have to do that, Laurel,' Finn said.

'They're good boys. They deserve a treat once in a while,' she said.

Doc Huntly cleared his throat. 'Nothing here for me to do. I'll be inside if anything comes up.'

'Come on, boy,' Webber said to Dan. 'Stuff to do at the office, I reckon.' He lifted his hat to Laurel. 'Thanks for coming in, Missus Baker. I'll ride out one of these days to have a look at your Rafter P on Paradise.'

'You're welcome, Marshal. Nothing fancy. My house burned down in August.'

Webber's eyes took on a sharp glint. 'Burned, you say?'

'Burned the same night my husband lost his life when something spooked his team off into Paradise Gorge. The four of us were doing OK at Paradise. . . .' Laurel's throat closed up. She swallowed hard. 'Now there's just me. My three men are buried on the hill,' she said, a tremble in her voice.

'Didn't know,' Webber said. 'I'll come pay my

110

respects soon as possible.'

'Thank you, Marshal. You come when you can.'

Webber tipped his hat again and walked back up the street toward the marshal's office with Dan Brady at his side.

'Riders coming,' Finn said.

Laurel shifted so her rifle covered the oncoming group of men, her knuckles white against the red of her healing burns as she clutched its stock.

Twenty yards away, the group slowed to a trot, then a walk. They kept their hands on their saddle horns. They stopped in front of Finn's mules.

'You got Red Finney,' asked a big white-haired man. 'Boss sent us to get him.'

'Back here,' Finn said from behind the wagon.

Laurel thumbed the hammer on the Winchester back to full cock. 'Two of you's enough,' she said. 'Two men put him in the wagon. Two can pull him out.'

'Don't get excited, ma'am,' Whitey said. 'We want no quarrel.'

'Fine,' she said, but didn't change the position of her Winchester.

'Bull, you and Taggart get Red. Put him on the extra horse and we'll get outta here.'

Two heavy-set men dismounted. One led a rider-less horse around to the back of Finn's wagon. Finn led the tailgate down.

'Jesus! What happened to him?'

'Tangled with a bear,' Finn said. 'Came up second best.'

'Where at?'

'Up on Paradise Creek.'

'She-it.'

'Take him away.' Finn sounded impatient. 'We gotta leave.'

The two men dragged Finney's body from the wagon and bent it over the saddle on the extra horse. They tied his hands and feet together under the horse's belly with a piggin string.

'Ready as we'll ever be, Dirk,' one said, leading the burdened horse back to the group.

'Let's go. Them other guys should have a place to plant him about dug,' Whitey said.

'You all be careful about who you send to Paradise to watch what's going on,' Finn called after the riders. 'We got nothing to hide, but we don't like people spying either. Next time it might not be a bear.'

Dirk Rawlins raised a hand without turning around. The riders took the road off the bluff down toward Bogtown.

'Finn, drive up to the marshal's office, please. I want to have a word with him,' said Laurel. 'We can pick the boys up on the way.'

Finn climbed up on the high seat, picked up the reins, and clucked at the mules. They put their shoulders to their collars and pulled the wagon down Main. 'Whoa up,' Finn said to the mules when they got to Gardner's Mercantile.

'Will. Cal! Time to move along,' Finn called. The boys ran from the general store with small paper

112

sacks of sweets in their hands. They scrambled into the wagon.

'Want a liquorice stick, Pa?' Will asked.

'What about Laurel?'

'I was gonna ask Laurel,' said Cal. 'Do you want one, Laurel. They're delicious good.'

Laurel laughed. 'Not right now, Cal, but thanks anyway.'

Finn clucked to the mules and drove the wagon to the marshal's office.

'Want me to come in with you?'

'No. This will take only a minute. Please stay here.' Laurel climbed down from the high seat, her Winchester under her arm and the Dragoon bulging in her mackinaw pocket.

Webber sat behind a big wooden desk.

'Marshal, I just need to say one thing to you, so you will know what's going on.' Laurel stood spraddle-legged in front of the desk, her rifle hanging in the crook of her arm, her hands clasped tightly together. The scar on her face flamed scarlet. She narrowed her eyes as she spoke. 'Robert Dunn has been out to my place on Paradise Creek twice. Once the day after my house burned down with my two sons in it and my husband dead at the bottom of Paradise Gorge.'

She stopped and took deep breath. Her voice scratched in her throat as she spoke. 'Then he came again a couple of weeks later and offered me a lot of money for my land. Dunn seems awful anxious to get the property, but I won't sell. My men are buried on that land.

Webber nodded. 'I can understand that,' he said.

'Now, I don't know why Red Finney was in the pines south of Rafter P in the middle of the night, but I doubt it was of his own accord. I imagine Robert Dunn will try to drive me off my land. Marshal, Dunn'd better not think he's going up against some weak pussyfooting woman, 'cause I'll fight.'

'Strictly speaking, Missus Baker, Paradise Valley is beyond my jurisdiction. I'm just the marshal of Ponderosa, which includes Bogtown. But I hear you, and I think you should be careful. Very careful.'

Laurel smiled stiffly and slapped the stock of her Winchester. 'We were born careful,' she said. She lifted a hand to Webber and left the office. She climbed up onto the wagon seat. 'Let's go home,' she said.

CHAPTER ELEVEN

The road back to Paradise seemed to lead on forever and the only sounds were the monotonous clip-clop of mule hoofs and the creaking and banging of the wagon. Finn didn't talk. Laurel thought his face looked grim. Jack would have told Laurel about the progress on their home, about the new calves, about the fresh-ploughed plots waiting for new seeds, about the elk that came to water at Paradise Creek in the early spring. Laurel loved to listen to Jack. She loved his vision of the future. She loved his concern for his sons. She loved his sturdy power and willingness to work. Perhaps most of all, she loved him for picking her, a blocky girl with freckles sprinkled across her face and none of the wasp-waisted multipetticoat femininity that most men seemed to like. She'd worn her dull brown hair in braids before that night. Now it hung ragged, covered mostly by her floppy hat. Laurel wrapped her arms around the Yellow Boy Winchester and rested her cheek against its cold barrel. The boys seemed to take a hint from their father and sat in the wagon bed in silence. Perhaps they'd fallen asleep.

As he reined the mule team onto the Paradise wagon track, Finn said. 'You know, I wonder.'

'Hmm?' Laurel's eyes remained closed.

'Laurel?'

'What?'

Finn shifted a little closer to her and spoke in a low voice. 'You know that dead man, Red Finney? I wonder where his horse is.'

'How would I know?'

'That's not what I mean. We found him dead, but it's not likely that he hiked all the way from Ponderosa. So his horse has to be around somewhere. When we get back, I'm gonna look for it.'

'OK.' Laurel closed her eyes again, still embracing the rifle. She didn't want to talk. She didn't want to cook. She just wanted it all to go away. A tear squeezed from the corner of her eye and followed the line of her scar as it trickled down her face.

Dirk Rawlins slammed his way through the batwing doors of Old Glory and strode to Robert Dunn's table. 'Red's buried,' he said.

Dunn poured a glassful of whiskey. 'For your extra effort,' he said, holding the drink out to Whitey.

The big man downed the whiskey in a single gulp. 'Good stuff,' he said, his eyes watering.

'What do you think, Dirk? Is there a way for me to get that land on Paradise? I've got to supply Comstock with two million board feet of round stock.

I can't do it without logging above Paradise.'

'What'll it take to scare 'em?'

Dunn put his head in his hands. 'I've tried being nice. I've tried to buy. That woman never even pretended to listen. Damn.'

Dirk moved his whiskey glass toward the bottle of Turley's mill.

'Pour it yourself. I'm not the bartender,' Dunn growled.

Dirk filled his glass, a big grin on his face. 'Maybe some potshots out of the woods would put a scare into her. Maybe hurt that man.'

'He's just a fence builder.'

'Yeah, but cutting him down would make her have to watch out for the buttons. Maybe she won't want to do that, her sons being dead and all.'

Dunn swallowed another gulp of Turley's Mill. 'You set it up, Dirk. I don't want to know.'

'Costs, Mr Dunn.'

'He's worth five hundred dead or hurt real bad.' Dunn dug five double eagles from his vest pocket. 'Here's a down payment,' he said. 'More when the job's done.'

Dirk tossed back a third glass of whiskey. 'Don't you worry about a thing, Mr Dunn. I'll wire Nathan Dyer. Ain't no one better at a long shot than him. He'd do it for three hundred, I reckon, along with a little travel money.'

'I didn't hear that. Don't tell me a thing. Just get the job done.'

*

117

Nathan Dyer rode into Ponderosa on a Saturday. The late September days were cool, and gold touched the leaves of the high-country aspen. A small man in a bowler hat, Dyer looked like a jockey atop his tall dark-brown Tennessee Pacer. A varnished cherrywood box hung from the saddle skirts by custom-made straps. Inside the case, Dyer carried a broken-down Pacific model Marlin-Ballard rifle barrelled by George Schoyen, an extra Schoyen barrel, a Sidle scope sight, and tools to load his own .32-.40 centrefire cartridges. Dyer preferred the smaller calibre as windage disturbed its flight less, and it travelled a flatter trajectory. With his carefully hand-loaded cartridges, Dyer could hit a target the size of a man's palm from 500 yards away. He didn't miss. In 1879, Dyer won the 800-yard shootout at the Spring Meeting of the Massachusetts Rifle Association at Walnut Hill in Woburn. He also found there was no money to be made hitting cast-iron targets from long distances. These days he used flesh-and-blood targets.

Dyer reined the Pacer up before Old Glory. He didn't like making deals in saloons and didn't drink himself. Alcohol ruined marksmanship. Nevertheless, Rawlins specified Old Glory. Dyer stepped down from the Tennessee Pacer and pushed his way through the batwing doors.

'Mr Dyer!' A large white-haired man in range clothes strode forward with his hand outstretched. 'I'm Dirk Rawlins,' he said. 'Come on over to my table.' He led the way to the back of the room.

Dirk motioned toward a seat. 'You can sit there,' he said.

Dyer quietly took the seat and surveyed the saloon. Long plank bar down one side of the room, backed by a flat mirror. Uneven floor of rough-sawn planks with sawdust scattered around. Spittoons by every table, six along the bar. Bottles of whiskey without labels on the shelf behind the bar. An open keg with a ladle handle protruding. Three men belly up to the bar. One man, apparently a card shark, idly playing solitaire at the middle table.

'Target?' Dyer asked.

'Drink?' Rawlins countered.

'Whiskey ruins my aim. Don't use it. Just give me a target, three hundred dollars, and fifty in travel expenses. I didn't come here to socialize.' Dyer's washed-out blue eyes held no expression.

'About a dozen miles east of here's a place called Paradise. It's really just a valley on Paradise Creek where a man named Jack Baker started a ranch with the Rafter P brand.'

'You want me to down Baker?'

'He died when we stampeded his team off the rim into Paradise Gorge at the north-west end of the valley. It's not him,' Dirk Rawlins said.

'Then who?'

'Just hold your horses. I'll get to it.'

Dyer leaned toward Rawlins. 'Pays to be quick about these things,' he said. 'I don't want to spend any more time in Ponderosa than I must, so get to it.'

'Baker had a wife and two sons, but the night his

119

team went off the cliff, his house burned. The boys were inside.'

'Hell of a way to get rid of a problem,' Dyer said. 'Not sure I like working for kid killers.'

'Accident. Their mom was supposed to get them out, but she was off gallivanting around trying to find her dead husband. Too bad.'

'Want me to down the woman?' Dyer spoke as if he had a sour taste in his mouth.

'No,' Rawlins said. He poured himself another whiskey and took a long drink. 'There's a fence builder on the place now, name of Finn McBride. Him being there's keeping the woman from folding. Need him out of action. Kill him if you have to, give him something he won't get over quick if you can.'

Dyer held his back straight. 'Mr Rawlins,' he said with a touch of pride in his voice, 'My bullets go where I aim them. If you wish McBride invalided, I'll make him so.'

'Then do it,' Rawlins said.

'The price is the same. Three hundred for the shot. Fifty for travel. I'll have it now, as I don't wish to be seen in this town again.'

Rawlins pulled a small leather poke from his pocket and plonked it on the table in front of Dyer. 'Three hundred and fifty in gold,' he said.

Dyer pocketed the poke without looking inside. 'How do I get to the target range?'

'Target range?'

'Yes. The site from which I am to hit the assigned target.' Dyer quickly scanned the room. No one seemed to be paying attention to him and Rawlins, but he didn't like to stay in a public place too long. 'Be specific,' he ordered.

Dirk Rawlins was at the whiskey again, though he didn't seem to be impaired. 'Ride east on Main Street. It will turn into the mail road to Alpine. About seven miles along, you'll see Paradise Gorge on your left.' Rawlins took another gulp.

'I'd say half a mile past the gorge you'll find a wagon track taking off to the left,' he said. 'Follow it. The remains of the ranch are on high ground some five miles along the track. You'll want to fade into the tree line on your right. Pick a good spot and take your shot.' Rawlins set the whiskey glass down with a loud clunk that made Dyer quickly glance about the room to see if the sound attracted attention. No one even looked up.

Jinx the bartender began setting out the free lunch, a tureen of potato soup, a round of roast beef, plenty of butter, and slices of bread. 'May I partake of the lunch?' Dyer asked.

'Help yourself before the crowd gets here,' Rawlins replied.

'But I don't drink.'

'I've drunk enough for both of us,' Rawlins said. 'Go ahead.'

Dyer buttered two slices of bread, placed several thin slices of beef between them, and ladled a bowl of soup from the tureen. He sat at the table and ate silently. When finished, he asked for a glass of water, drank it, and left the saloon. He had a target. Now to find the proper site for the shot.

At a running walk, Dyer's Pacer could do almost nine miles an hour, and keep it up all day. Dyer's line of work kept him on the road a lot, sometimes covering long distances. Over the years, he'd found Tennessee Pacers to have the easiest gate, even though the one he rode now stood nearly seventeen hands tall and made him look like a boy perched atop the saddle. When he bought it in Memphis, he just called the horse Pacer. Now the name had shortened to Pace, and the gentle gelding would follow Dyer like a dog if not told to 'stay'.

Before the ranch on Paradise came into sight, Dyer reined Pace south-east into the pine forest. The thick carpet of pine needles kept underbrush from taking over, except for the odd Manzanita. The small man on the big horse slipped quietly through the pines until he judged they were parallel with the ranch.

'Stay, Pace,' he said to the horse. He unbuckled the gun box from the saddle skirts and walked toward the edge of the forest. He crawled the last few yards until he could see down the slope toward Paradise Creek.

'Two-bit outfit,' he muttered. He put a clump of jack pines between himself and the ranch and proceeded to assemble the Marlin-Ballard. He affixed the 2x scope in place and picked a single .32-.40 cartridge from the box. He shined the bullet on his trouser leg, slipped it into the chamber, and locked the breech down. He moved forward on knees and elbows until he could see the ranch again.

As he watched, two boys ran off toward the barn. A man and a woman were in the burnt-out house, sitting before the still-standing fireplace. Dyer thought they were a mite too close together, but all he had to do was drop the man. He peered through the scope. It doubled the closeness of the image, and he could see warmth in the way the man looked at the woman. He thumbed back the hammer, muffling the click with his off hand, and settled into a spraddle-legged prone shooting position. Crosshairs on the man, Dyer took a deep breath, then let it half out. He started to tighten his finger on the trigger, then drew a sharp breath and stopped. Someone held the cold steel of a knife blade against his neck.

Lethargy dogged Laurel's life. She dragged through the days, said little, and spent hours each day on the hill sitting by Jack's grave. Finn took over as cook. He and the boys harvested the root crops, did the daily chores, caught fish at times, and once brought down a four-point buck mule deer to augment the meat supply. He'd found Finney's horse in the pines. Now it grazed in the paddock with Angel and Molly and Finn's mules.

Finn had cleaned out the house and placed cut-off log rounds as chairs around the fireplace, which was still standing. Now, instead of cooking and eating out in the yard, they did it by the hearth. Laurel liked to sit in quiet conversation with Finn after the boys had gone to bed. She hardly ever looked at him, but the deep rumble of his voice comforted her. And she couldn't help but notice how his square, work-roughened hands looked so much like Jack's. The gentleness of Jack's work-hardened hands had always been a thrill and a wonder to her.

Supper was over and the dishes washed. Evening chores kept the boys busy while Laurel and Finn sat in front of the fire on separate logs.

Finn's deep voice rumbled softly in the waning light. Laurel leaned toward him so she wouldn't miss any of the words. Their shoulders almost touched. 'Need to rebuild this house, Laurel,' he said. 'Foundation's firm. Lower logs didn't get burned, so rebuilding would be lots easier than starting fresh.' He got up to add a pitch-pine log to the fire. In a moment it caught and flared, and cast a warm yellow light on Laurel and Finn.

Laurel paused for a long moment. 'Finn,' she said, her voice soft and low in the twilight. 'I've not been fair to you. You hired on to build fences, but all you've been doing is housewife work. I'm sorry, Finn. I'll try to do my share.'

'Not to worry, Laurel,' he said. 'There's no one I'd rather work for, you know. And my boys think you're . . . just great.'

That brought a rare smile to Laurel's face. 'Just great, eh? I'll try to live up to that.' She fell silent, thinking of the man sitting beside her, so willing to bend so she could get over her losses. Another smile tugged at the corners of her mouth. Lucky she was to have this hired hand.

'What in Jesus' name?' Finn stared up the hill toward the forest. 'Look at that.'

Laurel reached for her rifle and turned to follow Finn's gaze. P'tone and Gondalay came from the forest. Gondalay led a tall brown horse and carried a strange rifle. P'tone held his knife against the neck of a small man in a bowler hat. A trickle of blood ran from under the edge of the knife. The little man's hands were tied behind his back. They walked in silence toward the burnt-out house and stopped just outside the remains of the wall.

'We watch,' P'tone said. 'This man came from Ponderosa way. He ride quiet. Walk quiet. Then he make a rifle from things in a box.'

'It's a free country,' the little man said. 'I can go where I want.'

'We watch. He watch, too. See boys go away. See two people sitting. He point rifle at two sitting people, woman from Dos Cabezas and new man.' P'tone waved a hand at the other Apache. 'Gondalay put knife on his neck. He don't shoot.'

P'tone pulled a poke from his loose shirt. 'He had this.'

'I was just perusing the country,' the man said. 'These savages don't know what they're talking about.'

P'tone pulled back slightly on the knife. New blood showed. The little man gasped and stopped talking.

Laurel eared back the hammer of her Yellow Boy. 'Mister, I don't know who you are or why you're here, but my friends don't lie. Come morning, we'll ride into Ponderosa and see what Marshal Webber has to say.'

CHAPTER TWELVE

Seth Owens showed up at Paradise in the early hours on Sunday. 'Oughta be going to church,' he said, 'but I got to thinking about Laurel and had to come down to see how she's doing.' He pointed to the small man sitting in Finn's wagon with his hands tied behind his back. 'Who's that?'

'Sharpshooter,' Finn said.

'Sharpshooter?'

'Some of my Apache friends found him at the edge of the pines in the evening, drawing bead on us,' Laurel said. 'We're taking him to Ponderosa to see Marshal Webber.'

'Mind if I come along?'

'You're welcome. Can Finn's boys ride in your wagon?'

'You bet.' Seth answered with his usual laugh.

A small cavalcade left Paradise for Ponderosa. Finn's wagon led. The little sharpshooter sat in the wagon bed, his hands still tied behind his back. The Tennessee Pacer ambled along behind the wagon, led by its reins tied to the tailgate. Red Finney's horse trotted on the other side. The sun rose bright as it did almost every day, and the morning chores were done in time to leave early. Laurel saw no sign of the Apaches, but she knew they watched, and she thanked God for her friends.

Laurel sat close to Finn McBride on the high seat. He drove the mules with casual grace, his work-hardened hands guiding the team. If Finn noticed that Laurel sat closer, he didn't say, but it seemed natural that way. She settled the Yellow Boy Winchester in the space between them, its butt on the floorboards and its barrel against the seat. 'Finn?' she said.

'Hmmm?'

'Does Dunn want Paradise bad enough to kill me?' Laurel glanced at Finn's face.

'With you dead, Paradise would be up for grabs. He seems to want the place bad. Could be that he had something to do with your Jack's death and maybe he lit the fire at the house.' Finn scratched at the stubble on his chin. 'Sorry I didn't get to shave this morning,' he said.

Laurel started to lift her hand, hesitated, then reached up to brush at his whiskers with her fingertips. 'Not all that bad,' she said. 'You worry too much.'

The two-wagon cavalcade reached Ponderosa late in the morning. Laurel noticed a woman watching them from the window of the *Examiner* building. She came out onto the boardwalk as the wagons came abreast of the newspaper, eyes on Dyer.

'Who's that in your wagon?' she asked.

'Sharpshooter,' Finn said.

The woman broke stride for a moment. 'What do you mean, sharpshooter?'

'Just what I said. He was laying out in the timber with a Marlin-Ballard sharpshooter rifle, figuring to drill me or Missus Baker here and sneak away.'

'Why?'

'I reckon someone hired him. He had three hundred and fifty dollars in gold on him.' Finn sounded like he had a bad taste in his mouth. 'We're gonna ask Marshal Webber.'

The two wagons continued up Main Street, passing the Comstock Hotel on their way to the marshal's office at the corner of Main and Ash. The woman from the *Examiner* kept pace.

Braxton Webber stood on the porch of the marshal's office as Finn's wagon pulled abreast.

'Whoa there,' Finn said, hauling back on the long leather reins.

'Marshal Webber,' Laurel called.

Webber tipped his hat. 'Missus Baker.'

Laurel thumbed at the little man sitting cross-legged in the wagon bed. 'Do you know this man?' She picked up the Marlin-Ballard from its place against the wagon side. 'He owns this.' She offered the sharpshooter rifle to the marshal.

'Well, well. A Marlin-Ballard.' The marshal unlocked the breech. 'Bullet still in it,' he mused. He opened the breech and caught the cartridge as it flipped up from the ejector. '.32-.40,' Webber said. 'Very expensive rifle. Ain't seen one of these since the

129

shooting matches at Prescott. Heard of people getting picked off by a sharpshooter in the Lincoln County war. Let me see who you've got there,' Webber said. He stepped up onto the iron stirrup people used to get into the wagon. He peered at the little man, who seemed to be trying to hide beneath his bowler hat. 'Still shooting for hire, Nathan Dyer?' he asked.

Dyer started.

'Have any money on him?' Webber asked Laurel.

'Three fifty in gold,' she said. She handed Webber the poke.

'Hmmm.' Webber pocketed the poke, lifted his hat, and smoothed back a shock of wavy brown hair. He set the hat on his head four square. 'Dyer, I'm going to arrest you for attempted murder.'

'I have shot no one,' Dyer said.

'Maybe not here,' Webber said, 'but I've got flyers in the office that say you're wanted in Wyoming and New Mexico. The US Marshal will be glad to take you to whoever wants you most. Now. Who hired you?'

Dyer clamped his mouth shut and stared at the wagon bed.

'Not saying, eh? Well, we'll just put you in the cell and wait to see who shows up.' Webber flipped the thong from his Colt Frontier .45 and drew the big revolver. 'Missus Baker. Could you have someone lower the tailgate on this wagon, please?'

'I'll do it,' Finn said. He vaulted off the high seat and untied the two horses. 'The tall one belongs to the sharpshooter,' he said to Webber. 'The other one was out in the pines alone. Red Finney's, I reckon.'

Webber nodded.

Finn tied the horses' reins to the hitching rail, then lowered the wagon tailgate.

Webber cocked his Colt. 'Come along, Dyer. Don't move sudden or you might get shot.'

Dyer slid across the wagon bed, let his legs hang over the edge, and stood up. He barely came to Webber's shoulder. The marshal took a handful of the sharpshooter's collar. 'Let's go,' he said and frog-marched Dyer into the office to lock him in one of the cells in the back.

The woman from the newspaper smoothed her blue gingham dress and stepped up on the porch to be on a level with Laurel. 'I'm Prudence Comstock,' she said to Laurel. 'I work at the *Examiner*, the newspaper here in Ponderosa. Could you tell me what happened?'

Laurel looked at Finn, but he was engrossed in raising the tailgate.

'Please,' Prudence said. 'May I invite you to dinner at Jimmy's Kitchen? We could talk there.'

'I'd have to bring Finn and his two sons, and our neighbor Seth Owens.'

The newspaperwoman winced, then put on a broad smile. 'That would be fine,' she said. 'I'd like to hear what everyone has to say.'

'Thank you. We accept,' Laurel said.

HIRED KILLER IN PARADISE.

It has come to the attention of this writer that heinous events have taken place at Paradise

Valley, just a few miles from our peaceful burg of Ponderosa. On 24 August, scarcely a month ago, Laurel Baker lost her husband and her boys. Somehow Jack Baker's team stampeded off the rim of Paradise Gorge. The fall broke Jack's neck and destroyed the horses. At about the same time, a suspicious fire broke out in the Baker house at the Rafter P ranch. Laurel Baker had ridden out to seek her husband, and so was absent when the fire began. Her sons, Jimmy and Jason, were lost in the fire.

The morning after brought Robert Dunn, logging magnate, to Paradise with two gunmen at his side. He hinted that he would buy the Rafter P from widow Baker at a reasonable price. The good widow declined and invited Dunn to leave her property or deal with the business end of her Winchester rifle.

Faced with working alone to harvest needed vegetables and grain for winter, widow Baker luckily was able to hire a male helper, Phineas McBride, and his two sons, Willard and Calvin. The widow lived in the tack room while the hired hands slept in the hayloft.

Widow Baker said a crippled black bear, which she named Slewfoot, often came to homesteads in the area looking for scraps. A few rounds fired in the air and a good shout usually caused Slewfoot to go back into the pine forest. Unknowingly, Slewfoot acted as bodyguard to widow Baker. Linus 'Red' Finney, a gunman in the hire of Robert Dunn, ran afoul of the bear in the midnight hours of 9 September. He wounded Slewfoot with a shot from his revolver, but paid for it with his life. Widow Baker and her hired hand brought the body to Ponderosa the next day.

Once more, according to the widow, Robert Dunn and his gunmen tried to get her to sell the ranch on Paradise. She refused, and Dunn warned her, she said, saying 'there are other ways.' Little did she realize that meant sending a sharpshooter to the Rafter P.

Said sharpshooter, one Nathan Dyer, was apprehended while taking aim at widow Baker and Mr McBride from a hideout amongst the pines. White Mountain Apaches, who are friends of the widow, keep watch in the forest at night. They detected the sharpshooter long before he had set up his blind. The Indians stopped Dyer before he could actually pull the trigger in the early-morning light, and took him to the Rafter P at knifepoint.

Dyer, who is wanted in both Wyoming and New Mexico, languishes in a cell at the Ponderosa Marshal's office. Marshal Webber has given widow Baker a voucher for the $500 reward on Dyer's head, and has sent word to US Marshal Meade to the effect that he has Dyer in custody.

One wonders who might have purchased the long-range shooting skills of a man like Nathan Dyer. One must also realize that only Robert

Dunn has shown undue interest in the Baker ranch. Furthermore, investigation by the *Examiner* shows that Dunn has failed to provide Comstock Log and Lumber Company with the contracted number of logs for its sawmill operation, and that the Great Western and Santa Fe railway is in the last phases of planning for a spur line to Ponderosa, which would, as laid out, run across the north-east corner of the Rafter P ranch. The railway has yet to begin negotiations with widow Baker for a right-of-way easement for the spur line. Might these facts have some bearing on Mr Dunn's actions?

'Damn. Damn. Damn. What's that crazy woman thinking? She's got no proof.' Dunn slammed his copy of the *Examiner* on the table.

'Dyer fell down on the job,' Rawlins said.

'Damn. I need those logs. I need the shorter run. Comstock's got me over a barrel. Double damn.'

'So what will you do about it?'

Dunn stared at Rawlins. The white-haired man was pushing hard, considering he was only a hired gun. Maybe he just wanted to go kill someone. 'What's it to you?' Dunn said.

'Simple. You get what you want, I get more of what I want.' Rawlins gave Dunn a feral smile. 'So how do we get what you want?'

'I need that Baker woman out of the way, along with her hired hand. Dyer was supposed to get rid of him.' Dunn sucked at his teeth. 'God, I'd like to wake up tomorrow and find Laurel Baker gone.'

'I could ride over to Round Valley and pick up some men who know how to use guns,' Rawlins said. 'I reckon a thousand dollars would get ten men for a few days of gun work.'

Dunn looked at Dirk Rawlins for a long moment. 'They get paid when the job's done,' he said. 'And they'd better be good.'

'If Gus Snyder at Outlaw Rook says they're good, they'll be good,' Rawlins said. 'Count on it.'

Dunn nodded. 'I've heard Snyder keeps his word.' He splashed a last shot of Turley's Mill in Rawlins' glass. 'Go the long way,' he said. 'Take Corduroy Road to Hondah and ride around through Vernon to Round Valley. Folks probably won't notice you've gone.'

Rawlins downed the whiskey and grinned. 'Be back in a couple of days, boss,' he said, 'with men and guns.' He strode from Old Glory and Dunn could hear his horse move down the road at an easy canter.

Dunn sighed. Why did things always seem to come down to killing? Why couldn't that stubborn woman just sell her miserable ranch to him? Damn. He took another drink. Rawlins would be back in a couple of days to solve his problem. With luck and a dozen gunhands, he wouldn't even have to leave town. He heaved himself to his feet and set out for Miss Murdock's Institute for Wayward Young Women. He needed something to take his mind off Laurel Baker. Bucktooth Alice would be just the trick.

*

'Finn, we need supplies,' Laurel said. He stopped the wagon in front of Gardner's mercantile. Laurel climbed down from the high seat and walked into the store with her Yellow Boy Winchester in hand.

'Mr Gardner,' she called.

The greying owner came from the back. 'Good day, Missus Baker. Anything special I can do for you today?'

'Finn?'

'I'm here,' the hired man said. He carried a pair of saddle-bags.

'Mr Gardner, is my credit good?' Laurel asked. 'I didn't bring any cash with me today.'

'Of course. What can I get for you?'

'Just a few things. We need a sack of flour, one of pinto beans, and a side of bacon, if you've got one.'

'That's no problem, Missus Baker.'

'Laurel,' Finn said, 'I should practice with my short gun and I'm almost out of cartridges. Would it be all right to get a couple of boxes of .44-.40s?'

'Mr Gardner?'

'Yes, I have that calibre.'

'And a box of .22 long rifle for the varmit gun,' Finn said.

'Certainly. Will that be all?' The storekeeper piled Laurel's purchases on the counter.

'Will? Cal?' Laurel called for Finn's sons, who came scrambling in from outside. 'You may have a small sack of hardtack,' she said, 'but you must share evenly.'

'Yes, ma'am,' they chorused.

Finn stuffed the ammunition into the saddle-bags and returned to the wagon to let down the tailgate. Laurel signed the bill.

'I'll bring the money next time I come to town,' she said.

'When you can, Missus Baker. I know you're good for it.'

'Thank you.'

Finn returned first for the flour and again for the beans and bacon.

As Finn's wagon rolled out of Ponderosa with Seth Owens's following along behind, he leaned toward Laurel. 'With all the shooters showing up around Paradise, I figured to do some practising with my revolver. I'll pay you for the cartridges.'

'You don't have to do that. It comes with riding for the brand,' Laurel said.

She sat quietly on the high seat while Finn drove the wagon. Will and Cal jostled and played in the wagon bed. The wagon rolled along the rim of Paradise Gorge. At the turnoff, she could see across the valley. Paradise Creek ran silver through the meadows. The barn was a black blotch at the far end.

'Finn,' she said. 'I must be ready for anything, and I have no idea what Dunn will do. I hope you'll stand with me, but I'll understand if you and the boys decide to move on.'

Finn took a deep breath and put his hand on hers. 'Laurel, you can always depend on me,' he said.

CHAPTER THIRTEEN

Seth Owens drove on home, saying Priscilla expected him by dark. Finn chopped firewood and Cal carried it to the fireplace. Will built the fire, starting with kindling and split pieces. Laurel fixed biscuits. Venison and onions and potatoes from the root cellar, fried golden brown, made their supper. The group said little, fatigue from the trip to Ponderosa limited the conversation.

When supper was served, everybody bowed their heads while Laurel said, 'Dear God, thank you for this food. May it give us the strength we need. Amen.'

The boys glanced first at Finn, then at Laurel. No one spoke, so they concentrated on eating. When they finished, Will looked at Laurel from beneath his eyebrows.

'Laurel,' he said. 'You sure cook good.'

'Why thank you, Will,' Laurel said.

Will blushed and ducked his head.

'Put your dishes in the dishpan,' Laurel said, 'and

get on to bed. Tomorrow starts early enough.'

'Yes, ma'am,' the boys chorused and scrambled to do what Laurel asked.

The man and the woman sat on chunks of wood in front of the fireplace. Smoke issued from the chimney that stood alone amidst the remains of Laurel's home. They said nothing, but the silence seemed warm to Laurel. She felt that Finn understood her and she him. At last she stretched her arms above her head.

'It's been a long day,' she said. 'I think I'll turn in.'

Finn smiled. 'Sleep well,' he said. 'I'll stay up a little longer. Maybe have a look around.'

'P'tone and his men are watching,' she said.

'Yes. They'll take care of the forest. I'll look out for the Rafter P.'

'Oh. OK. Good night.' Laurel picked up her Yellow Boy, checked the cartridge in the chamber, then walked to the tack room with the rifle held ready. She shut and barred the door, then leaned the rifle against the wall. She knew the tack room well and didn't need to light a lantern. Her mackinaw went on a peg in the wall. The box bed creaked as she sat to remove her boots and socks. She took off her old cut-down jeans, folded them by feel, and put them on top of the chest next to the bed. Her shirt was also a cut-down, flannel and warm for autumn. She placed it atop the jeans. With a sigh, she lay back on the straw tick and pulled up a woollen blanket to cover her. In moments she was asleep.

Laurel's eyelids sprang open with the first shot. She scrambled for her clothes, jerked them on, and jammed her feet into her boots.

Shots sounded almost without interval.

She snatched up the Yellow Boy. With her hand over the action to muffle the sound, she pulled the hammer back to full cock.

Another volley of shots roared from down by the creek.

Laurel slid the bar from its slot in the wall. Now the door would open quickly and quietly. She squatted before the door, planning her rolling exit.

A third volley began.

Laurel burst through the door, moving low and fast, rolling on her shoulder and ending up flat on the ground with her rifle pointing toward the creek.

A can bounced and jumped as bullets from Finn's Colt .44 slammed into it. When the sixth shot smashed into the can, Finn relaxed and started ejecting the spent brass from the pistol. A cloud of black powder smoke hung over the creek.

'Finn McBride!' Laurel shouted. She left the Yellow Boy on the ground as she jumped up and ran downhill toward Finn as fast as she could. She crashed into him full tilt, saving herself from falling by wrapping her arms around his waist. Once her pell-mell dash was finished, Laurel released Finn and took a step back. Starting at the tops of her boots, she swung a doubled-up fist that caught Finn high on his left cheekbone.

'Damn you, Finn McBride!' She moved in closer,

pummelling Finn's chest with her fists. 'Damn you.' Tears streamed from her eyes and she put her head against his chest as she beat at his ribs. Her arms seemed to lose power. And she ended up with her arms around Finn's waist again as she bawled tears of pain and frustration.

'I-I-I thought they'd come shooting. I thought maybe you were dead. I couldn't stand it. I can't stand it. Finn, I don't want you to die.'

Finn gently wrapped his arms around her. 'Easy, lass. No one's killed me. I don't die so easy.' He kissed the top of her head through her tousled hair.

Her arms went up around his neck. She lifted her face to look at Finn through eyes swimming with tears. 'Don't leave me, Finn,' she said.

Finn kissed her upturned lips. Just a brush. Tenderly. 'Trust me, Laurel. I won't leave you. And I'll not let anyone harm you.'

He took her shoulders in his hands and stood her away from him. 'Now,' he said. 'I said yesterday I needed to practise with my pistol.' Finn grinned. He held out the Colt. 'At least I know it shoots where I point it.'

Finn ejected the remaining spent shells and refilled the chambers from the gunbelt around his hips. The belt was old but well cared for; its loops held new .44-.40 cartridges. Laurel saw that Finn was completely comfortable with the rig.

He picked another can and tossed it about twenty-five feet away. As the can hit the ground, Finn drew his revolver, thumbing back the hammer as he cleared the holster and triggering the gun when it pointed at the can. The can jumped, a hole torn in its side. Finn cocked and triggered the Colt smoothly and quickly, and each bullet gouged metal from the can. After six shots, little remained.

'You're quite good with that Colt,' Laurel said, sniffing and wiping at her wet face with her shirt-sleeve.

Finn smiled. 'A lifetime ago I was very good. Now it's time to polish up those old skills. This time, maybe shooting well will help me protect what I love.' He turned his attention to reloading the revolver. He shoved it into the holster and strode toward the horse paddock.

'Time to get some wood for winter,' he said. 'I saw a likely windfall in the pines. I'll take the mules and drag it in.'

'You'd better eat breakfast first,' Laurel said.

'It's not far off. I can get it while you're frying eggs.'

Laurel laughed, and wiped away the last of her tears. 'Whatever you say. Don't blame me if your food gets cold.'

Just as Laurel was dishing up fried potatoes and topping them with eggs, Finn came out of the pines with the traces of his big Missouri mules hitched to an old pine log about thirty inches in diameter at the base and about fifteen feet long to where Finn had sawn it off. He swerved the team so the log swung parallel to the wagon track with its end close to the burnt-out wall of the house.

'Whoa up,' Finn commanded, and the mules stopped straining at their collars. 'Good boys,' he said, patting each on the neck and rubbing their noses.

'Breakfast is on,' Laurel called.

'Be there in a minute,' he said.

'We're coming,' Will shouted from the chicken coop.

Minutes later, the McBride men were seated on rounds of wood, their food on plates in their laps. They waited for Laurel to say grace, then dug into the food as if they were starving.

'Today we'll drag windfalls over so we'll have fuel for winter,' Finn said. 'Will, you bring an axe and Cal can bring the hatchet. Trim the branches off the trunks, and Frank and Jesse Mule will drag in the logs.'

'Frank and Jesse?' Laurel said.

Finn grinned. 'Those critters are the worst outlaws in muledom, so I named them Frank and Jesse, after the James brothers.'

'I've never heard you call them by name,' she said.

'They're sensitive beasts,' said Finn. 'They don't like those names very much, having never committed a crime, so mostly I don't bother.'

Laurel stamped her foot. 'Finn McBride. If you're going to name your animals, give them something worthwhile. Now get on with it. I've dishes to do and clothes to wash. We've been too long without a bath and a change.'

Finn laughed deep in his chest. 'Oh my. Yes indeed, Laurel. Yes indeed.' He called to the boys. 'Did you hear Laurel, my sons? A bath in the creek when we finish work today. Time to wash off a bit of that grime clinging to your faces.'

'Ah, Pa. The creek's cold.' Cal griped about the coming bath.

'A bit of cold water and hard soap is good for a growing boy,' Finn said. 'Now let's go get those wind-falls.'

By suppertime, a respectable pile of windfall wood lay stacked between the house ruins and the tack room. While she worked, Laurel also fed Finn and the boys biscuits and bacon for dinner. They ate the food on the fly, washing it down with cold spring water.

Laurel put a pot of pinto beans on the stove with chunks of venison, pieces of carrot, slices of onion, salt, and a generous portion of dried and pounded chili. It simmered all afternoon as she washed clothes and took a bath in the creek while the McBrides were away in the forest. She had no tortillas, so she fixed thin frybread instead.

'Go bathe,' she said. 'Soap down good and use the washcloths to scrub the dirt off. I put out clean clothes for you. When you're finished, we'll eat.'

Laurel turned her back on the men as they stripped and plunged into Paradise Creek just upstream of the horse paddock. They came to the fire rubbing their wet hair with towels and shining with newly washed cleanliness. Laurel handed them dishes of chili and palm-sized pieces of frybread. Red Finney and the sharpshooter Nathan Dyer and the possibility that Robert Dunn would take drastic steps to get Paradise Valley faded for the moment as Laurel and the McBrides enjoyed their meal.

Day settled quietly into night. Small sounds – the cricket chirping under the tack room, the bullfrog's croak from down the creek, a faint whoo-whoo from a barred owl amongst the pines. A calf bumped its head against the gate to the cow pen, unhappy that it was separated from its mother. Laurel slipped into slumber without realizing it. She and the men slept until sunrise. Four Apache warriors slipped over the ridge toward the reservation as a line of grey showed in the east. Nothing awry in Paradise.

Under cover of darkness, eleven men walked their horses up Corduroy Road to Bogtown and let the mounts into the corral behind Old Glory. Each man carried his weapons of choice, mainly Winchester rifles and Colt revolvers, with the occasional Remington or Smith & Wesson.

'You all stay out here until I find Dunn,' said Dirk Rawlins. 'I'll be back shortly.' He strode into the saloon through the back door. As he expected, Robert Dunn sat at the rear table with a bottle of Turley's Mill and a glass with two fingers of amber whiskey in it. When he saw Dirk, Dunn downed the whiskey and wiped at his mouth with the back of his hand. The corners of his mouth pulled downward.

'They're here,' Rawlins said.

Dunn took a deep breath, held it, then let the air whistle out between his teeth. 'Good,' he said. It almost sounded like he meant it.

'We can still call them off,' Rawlins said. 'Just pay them a bit for the ride and maybe a poke or two at Miss Murdock's. But if you send them to Paradise, they insist on you riding along.'

Dunn straightened in his chair. 'Gotta take care of the Paradise problem once and for all. I'll be right out.' He called to the bartender.

'Leaving for a while, Jinx. Look after my bottle.'

'Yes, sir, Mr Dunn.' Jinx moved out from behind the bar and strolled over to Dunn's table, wiping his hands on the soiled white apron tied around his hips. He took the bottle, jammed the cork down hard with the palm of his right hand, and returned to the bar. He put Dunn's bottle out of sight in the hutch. 'Don't you worry about a thing, Mr Dunn,' he said. 'It'll be here when you want it.'

Dunn nodded. He followed Rawlins out the back door.

Dan Brady burst into the marshal's office. 'Marshal! Marshal! I seen 'em. A whole bunch of 'em.'

'Just slow down, Dan. Take some time. Get your breath.' Webber waited until Dan stopped panting. 'Sit down,' he said. 'Now, what did you want to tell me?'

Dan took a deep breath. 'I was walking around over in Bogtown,' he said. 'Just making sure things was quiet and all.'

Webber heaved a sigh. 'Dan, my boy, how many times to I have to tell you not to wander around at night. Some drunk might make a mistake and kill you.'

Dan stared at the floor. After a moment he said, 'I know I'm not a deputy, Marshal. I know. But someday I maybe will be, and I need to understand what to do beforehand. Can I tell you what I seen?'

The marshal sat back in his chair. 'Go ahead,' he said.

'I was walking down Corduroy Road, Marshal, when I heard a bunch of horses coming up the road. I slipped into the shadows and watched Dirk Rawlins lead ten men to the horse corral back of Old Glory.'

'Ten men, eh?'

'Yes, sir. I hung around, but when Mr Dunn come out the back to talk with those owlhoots, I skedaddled up here to tell you.'

'Hear anything Dunn had to say?'

'No, sir. But I recognized two of those men. Kid Crandall and Shotgun Lou Grimes. I reckon the others are gunmen, too, by the looks of their hardware.'

'Hmmm.' Webber pulled a double-barrelled ten-gauge from the gun cabinet, then reached into a drawer beneath the cabinet gun rack for a box of shotgun shells. He put two in the gun and snapped it shut, then stuffed a handful in his coat pocket. 'You stay here,' he said to Dan, and disappeared into the night.

At first, Dan sat in the marshal's chair with a

Winchester rifle across his knees. He had no watch, and the office had no clock. Time passed as if dragged by logging chains. He stood and walked to the window, but could see nothing. He went outside.

The buildings along Main Street were dark. Dan walked across the street to the corner of Main and Corduroy Road. From the high ground, he looked across Bogtown. Coal-oil lanterns lit windows in Old Glory, Charlie's Place, Miss Murdock's, and some of the shacks across the way. He saw no sign of Marshal Webber. He heard no drunken shouts or quarrelling. Soldiers from Camp Kinishba were not in town, and payday at the sawmill was still three days away. Few had extra cash to spend at saloons or brothels. Dan heaved a sigh and returned to the office.

The youngster sat again in the marshal's chair with the Winchester across his knees. Silence filled the room, broken once in a while by a snort from the sharpshooter sleeping in a holding cell in back. Dan leaned back in the chair and closed his eyes for a moment. He slept.

'Dan!' Marshal Webber's voice shook the teenager awake. 'Come out here.'

Dan stumbled from the office onto the porch. The east greyed with false dawn.

Marshal Webber held the reins to Nathan Dyer's Tennessee Pacer. 'This is the fastest horse around over a long haul,' he said. 'Get up on him and make for Paradise Valley. Tell Laurel Baker and Finn McBride that gunmen are headed their way. Tell them to get ready.' The marshal smashed the flat of his hand against the hitching rail. 'The Rafter P is out of my jurisdiction,' he said, 'but that doesn't mean I can't warn those folks. Ride, boy.'

CHAPTER FOURTEEN

Laurel stopped stirring the eggs. 'Horse coming,' she said. She set the frying pan aside and picked up her Yellow Boy Winchester.

Finn pulled his Colt. 'Get behind the woodpile, boys,' he said. Will and Cal ran out of the ruined house and sat down with their backs to the pine windfalls they'd helped drag in the day before.

'Missus Baker, Missus Baker!'

'Here,' Laurel called.

Dan Brady came into sight, mounted on the sharp-shooter's Tennessee Pacer, which was moving smartly at a running walk. 'Marshal Webber sent me, Missus Baker,' he called as he reined the Pacer to a stop.

'Doesn't sound like good news,' Laurel said.

'No, ma'am. It ain't. Mr Dunn and Dirk Rawlins and a bunch of Round Valley gunmen rode out of Ponderosa this morning. Marshal Webber said to warn you. I reckon you can expect gunplay. I'd help, ma'am, but I ain't got a gun.'

'Take this,' Laurel said, pulling the old Dragoon .45 from her mackinaw pocket and handing it up to Dan. She added a handful of cartridges, which he put in his coat pocket. 'The gun's yours, Dan. Now I'd like to ask you a favour.'

He turned the old revolver over in his hand. 'Yes, ma'am. And thank you. I'll treat it right.'

'Ride on up the wagon track, over the ridge, and into the next swale to Seth Owens's homestead. Tell him what's happening.'

'Yes, ma'am, I'll do that.' Dan clucked to the Pacer and slapped his heels against its sides. The tall horse was off and moving away at a rapid four-beat running walk.

Laurel turned to Finn. 'What can we do? There are so many.'

'Cut down the odds. Do something they don't expect.' Finn frowned as he considered the situation. 'Can you smoke, Laurel?'

'What kind of question is that?'

'For what I'm thinking, you'll need to keep a cigar alight. I'll be back in a moment,' he said, and ran to the barn. He disappeared inside and reappeared moments later carrying a small box, which he set down behind the pile of windfall logs near the ruins of the house. 'Come here, Laurel,' he said as he opened the box and took out a waxpaper-wrapped stick about an inch thick and eight inches long.

'I use this Giant Powder when I'm making post-holes in malpais or hard clay,' he said. 'I'll give you a ten-second fuse on each.' He cut the fuse at the second white dot on the length of fuse. 'Only five sticks left, but they'll help.'

Finn extracted a cigar can from the box, and took out a three-inch cheroot. 'When we hear them coming, light the smoke.' He handed her three lucifers.

'You'll sit here, with your back against the logs. I'll go out and stop the shooters. When I holler "Now," light a fuse, hold it for a second, then loft it over your head toward the riders.'

'I don't want to hurt the horses.' Laurel said.

'Honey. We've got to win. We've got to keep them from killing you and taking the Rafter P. If we have to wound or kill a horse, so be it. Can you do what I've asked?'

Laurel nodded, tears forming in her eyes. She clamped her jaws shut and brushed her face with a sleeve. 'I'll do what I have to,' she said.

'Good.'

Finn called to his boys. 'Will. Cal. There's going to be some shooting going on, so I want you two to get into the barn. Will, you get the shotgun, and Cal, you the .22.'

'Yes, Pa,' Will said. 'Come on, Cal.'

'Get into the last stall, away from the barn door, and don't shoot unless someone you don't know tries to get into your stall. Got that?'

'Yes, Pa.'

'Then git.'

The boys raced for the barn.

'Here they come,' Finn said.

Laurel stood and looked down the wagon track. A line of horsemen trotted toward the Rafter P. Robert Dunn rode fifth from the left so he had four riders on the forest side. Seven more gunslingers rode on the creek side. Each carried a Winchester in the right hand, butt on thigh and muzzle pointing skyward.

Finn stepped out onto the wagon track. His fawn-coloured gunbelt looked incongruous with his bib overalls, but it rode comfortably around his hips. He tipped his hat down to cover his eyes. Laurel dropped behind the windfall logs. She got a cheroot from the tobacco tin and lit it. She stuck the lucifer into the ground as she puffed the smoke alight. Acrid smoke attacked her membranes and threatened to make her cough. She held the impulse down. The tip of the cheroot glowed.

She lined the sticks of Giant Powder in a row at her right hand. Ten seconds from fuse light to explosion. She drew at the cheroot again.

'I'm going,' Finn said, and turned to face the oncoming riders.

Laurel hunched down behind the logs and puffed at the cheroot. The five sticks of Giant Powder lay in a line within easy reach. She picked one up and waited. The sound of walking horses came from down the wagon track.

'You brought a bunch of gunmen with you, Mr Dunn,' Finn's voice said. 'Doesn't seem like a friendly visit.'

'Where's Missus Baker?' It was Dunn who spoke.

153

'You want to say something, talk to me.'

'I had my say to Missus Baker, by God,' Dunn shouted. 'If she's not gonna take my offer of gold, I'm here to make one in lead.'

A clatter of clicks as the gunmen cocked their rifles was followed immediately by the bellow of Finn McBride's revolver. Three shots so close together they sounded like one. 'Now, Laurel,' he shouted. Winchesters cracked.

Laurel stuck the glowing end of the cheroot to the Giant Powder stick's fuse, waited a second to make sure it was lit, and threw it back over her head, arching it up high in the air to come down in the middle of the wagon track. A second and a half after it hit the ground, the Giant Powder exploded. A horse screamed. Men shouted. Finn's pistol barked twice more. Laurel lit another fuse with shaking hands. She held the stick longer this time. One . . . two . . . three . . . then lobbed it so the powder stick would hit about ten feet farther up the wagon track. This time the explosion came before the stick hit the ground. Laurel could hear the ungh-ungh-ungh of bucking horses. Finn shot again, followed immediately by the crack of a Winchester. Finn grunted. Laurel lit and lobbed a third stick of Giant Powder, grabbing up her rifle as the stick flew through the air. She sat still until the stick exploded, then crawled to the north end of the windfall stack, cheroot clamped in her teeth.

Horses still bucked, three without riders. The gunmen had sought cover in the pines. Robert Dunn

154

lay spread-eagled in the middle of the wagon track. Dirk Rawlins dragged himself towards the tree line, but his strength gave out. He lay still with a swath of blood painted on the track beneath him. His white hair ruffled in the breeze.

Two gunmen bled on ground broken by Giant Powder blasts. One made no move. One groaned. The battleground was silent.

'Finn? Finn? Are you there?' Laurel's voice quavered with stress. She inched a little farther out from behind the windfall pile. A bullet crashed into a log not two inches from her head. She scrambled back behind the windfall logs.

'Finn?'

No answer.

The four-beat sound of a running horse came from up the track. A rifle spat from the tree line. Another from a mound on the far side of the barn. Laurel aimed at the rounded top of a hat she could see sticking up from the mound and gently pulled the trigger. Dirt flew from the mound, and her bullet screamed off down the valley.

Dan Brady let go of the saddle horn and dropped from his one-stirrup hold on the far side as the Tennessee Pacer plunged past the windfall. 'Barn,' Dan shouted at the horse, which obediently made its way through the open barn door. Dan grabbed the Dragoon from his waistband, cocked the big Colt and stood straight up. He immediately dropped and rifle fire tore chips from the windfall and thumped into big old logs. 'Had to see where they was,' Dan said, a big grin on his face.

'I saw Dunn and Rawlins down. A couple of riders I didn't know,' Laurel said.

'That means Kid Crandall and Shotgun Lou Grimes are still out there. Four down. Eight to go. Don't like the odds. How's Mr McBride?'

'I called for him. No answer.'

'Shit. Excuse my language, ma'am.'

The throaty roar of a buffalo gun came from the ridge at the south-east end of Paradise Valley. A shower of debris flew from the top of the mound of earth on the far side of the barn, a hat tumbled away, its crown ripped open to the brim.

'That'll be Mr Owens,' Dan said. 'He said he'd be along as soon as he could get his Sharps .50-.90. Him and Billy Dixon and them other old boys held Injuns off to nearly a mile away in the Buffalo Wallow fight. I heard about that.'

The Sharps roared again. A man in the pines screamed. 'Holy, holy . . . my arm . . . my arm . . . it's gone. Help, for gawdsake, help! Ahgh. Ahgh. Aaaaaagh.'

Dan Brady crept to the north end of the windfall, the Dragoon in his left hand. He peered around the edge of the logs. After a moment he said, 'I think I can see Mr McBride. He's down behind a tree. Ain't moving. I'd better go see what's the matter.'

'Dan! You can't just walk across the road. They'll shoot you dead.'

'Not if you cover me.' Dan waved a hand at Laurel's rifle. 'And I'll run, not walk.'

Laurel nodded, a grim look on her face. She puffed at the cheroot and reached for a Giant Powder stick. 'This goes off 10 seconds after I light it,' she said. 'Get ready.' She touched the fuse to the end of the cheroot, waited for a second to make sure the fuse lit, then tossed it as far into the trees as she could.

Dan sprinted from behind the windfall pile as the Giant Powder stick exploded. Laurel jumped to her feet, her rifle at her shoulder. She levered the action and pulled the trigger as fast as she could, spraying bullets through the trees. The buffalo gun roared from the ridge. A few seconds later, it roared again.

Dan slid to his knees beside the thick trunk of an old Ponderosa. Laurel lit the last stick of Giant Powder and flung it into the woods. 'Heads down!' she shouted and dropped behind the windfall. The sound of a tree toppling followed the explosion.

'Missus Baker?'

Laurel's knuckles were white as she gripped her rifle, but she said nothing.

'Missus Baker?'

Laurel heaved a sigh. 'What do you want?' Her voice cracked.

'We're just hired hands, Missus. Man who did the hiring's dead. If it's just the same with you, call off the buffalo hunter, quit heaving Giant Powder, and we'll leave. We'll not bother you again.'

'Where's Finn?'

A weak voice came from back in the pines. 'I'm here, Laurel. Dan's got me covered. Let them ride out. Leave the wounded. We can take them all to Ponderosa to Doc Huntly.'

'Did you hear Mr McBride?' Laurel shouted. 'Leave everything as it is and ride away.'

'Tell the buffalo hunter.'

Laurel stood up and laid her Yellow Boy against the windfall pile. She held her hands at shoulder level. She walked to the middle of the wagon track and kicked at Robert Dunn with the toe of her boot. His arm flopped. Dead. She turned to face up the wagon track. 'Seth?'

'I hear you, Laurel.'

'The gunmen say they'll leave. Don't shoot unless they don't keep their word.'

'Seth Owens?' A short man with bowed legs and leather chaps walked out onto the wagon track. He carried a shotgun with the action broken open. 'I'm Lou Grimes. I told Missus Baker we'd go; I keep my word.'

'Lou Grimes, eh? Heard you're a man who keeps his word. Didn't you say you'd kill this young widow?'

Grimes kicked at a clod. 'I did,' he said reluctantly, 'but the man I promised is dead. I'm free to say something else.'

'All right, Lou. Take them gunmen and ride away. I'll stay here. You know I can hit anything within a mile, so be careful.'

'Men,' Grimes called. 'Come out. Get your horses. Ride away. We ain't never coming to Paradise again.'

Laurel didn't wait for the gunmen to leave. She hurried into the pines. 'Finn? Finn? Are you all right?

Finn!' Her voice carried a shrill note of panic.

She found him sitting spraddle-legged with his back against a tree. Sweat rolled down his face. Blood covered his shirt and soaked through his bib overalls. He gave her a feeble smile. 'The Giant Powder worked,' he said. 'Dunn's no problem, nor is Dirk Rawlins, though he got lead into me. Give me an arm up. I'll walk home.'

'You'll do no such thing,' Laurel said. She shed her mackinaw and ripped off her shirt. She tore the shirt into strips and pieces, made a pad, then tied it over the wound with the strips. 'Entry wound only,' she said. 'We've got to get you to Doc Huntly so the bullet can come out.'

'Seth!' she screamed. 'You and Dan get Finn to the wagon track,' she said, then ran for the barn.

'Will. Cal. Come out. Come here,' she shouted.

She gathered the two boys in her arms when they ran from the barn. 'Your father is hurt. We must take him to Ponderosa. Will, can you get Frank and Jesse? Can you harness them and hitch them to the wagon?'

'I'll do it, Laurel,' Will said, 'and Cal can help.'

By the time Dan and Seth got Finn ready to go, the mules were harnessed and in their traces. Laurel gave Dan a pad of flour sacking and told him to hold it to Finn's wound. 'I can do that,' Will said. 'He's my pa.'

Laurel drove Frank and Jesse as fast as the two mules would move. She cracked the whip about their ears and screamed at them to go faster. Seth Owens followed, his wagon carrying the dead and wounded. They made record time to Ponderosa.

*

Finn was still under chloroform when Braxton Webber arrived. 'Wanna tell me what happened?' he said.

Laurel related the events of the morning in a soft monotone. 'Robert Dunn came to take my land by force,' she said at last. 'I wouldn't have it. Finn stood up to him and his killers.' A tear rolled down her cheek and across the scar along her jawbone. 'Now Finn McBride may die.' She sobbed. 'Marshal, please take those dead men away,' she said.

As Webber was leaving, Doc Huntly came in. 'Got the bullet out. Repaired the damage. Cleaned him out good. Now it's up to him.'

Laurel gathered Finn's sons to her. 'Come on, boys. Your father needs you.' She led them into Finn's room. 'Now for those gunsharps,' she heard Doc Huntly say, but her attention was focused on Finn McBride.

Laurel and the boys waited. As the evening deepened and the nurse came in to light the coal-oil lamps, Finn's eyes opened. 'Laurel,' he said. 'Boys.' He stretched an arm in their direction.

'It's about time you woke up, Finn McBride. Lots of things need doing on the Rafter P, and you're lazying around in bed.' Laurel squeezed Finn's extended hand.

'You mean I still have a job?'

'For as long as you want,' she said, and kissed him. 'But don't you ever scare me like that again.'